1/10

D0325032

Birdie For Now

ORCA
YOUNG
READERS

Birdie
for Now

Jean Little

ORCA BOOK PUBLISHERS

Copyright © 2002 Jean Little

All rights reserved. No part of this publication may be reproduced or transmitted in any form or by any means, electronic or mechanical, including photocopying, recording or by any information storage and retrieval system now known or to be invented, without permission in writing from the publisher.

National Library of Canada Cataloguing in Publication Data

Little, Jean, 1932-

Birdie for now

ISBN 1-55143-203-X

I. Title. PS8523.I77B57 2002   jC813'.54   C2002-910032-1

PZ7.L7225Bi 2002

Library of Congress Catalog Card Number: 2002100303

Orca Book Publishers gratefully acknowledges the support for its publishing programs provided by the following agencies: the Government of Canada through the Department of Canadian Heritage's Book Publishing Industry Development Program (BPIDP), the Canada Council for the Arts, and the British Columbia Arts Council.

Cover design by Christine Toller
Cover & interior illustrations by Renné Benoit

Printed and bound in Canada

IN CANADA	**IN THE UNITED STATES**
Orca Book Publishers	Orca Book Publishers
1030 North Park Street	PO Box 468
Victoria, BC Canada	Custer, WA USA
V8T 1C6	98240-0468

07 06 05 04 • 6 5 4 3

This story is for Ben and Jeanie; Ian and Douglas; Angus, Jack, Daniel and Katie; Melanie and Emilie; Liam and Sebastian; and Hugh and Donnie, with my love.

My affectionate thanks also go to Susan Milton, who introduced me to Toby and Panda, my Papillons, without whom Birdie would never have lived.

J.L.

Table of Contents

Left Behind

Dickon Fielding hurtled down the stairs that Saturday morning, still in pajamas. His feet were bare. His fair hair, which usually hung down smoothly to his eyebrows, was on end. And his dark eyes behind his glasses were anxious.

What if she had slept in? He jumped the last two steps and skidded to a stop.

But his mother was wide awake. Gazing sideways out the kitchen window, she stood and sipped her morning coffee.

"When do we leave?" he yelled, his voice shattering the silence, his body bouncing up and down like a Nerf ball.

She turned her head.

"You need your hair cut," she said.

Then she gulped down the last of her coffee and busied herself at the sink.

Something was wrong. No empty coffee cup needed that much rinsing. He sidestepped, trying to see her expression.

"Mum?" he began.

Then the truth hit him. She was going without him.

She turned in time to catch the shock on his face.

"Birdie darling, don't look like that," she began, reaching out to smooth his hair and straighten his glasses.

She tried to sound ordinary, but her words stumbled and jumped like bare feet on sharp stones. Her cheeks were a tattle-tale pink and she did not look him in the eye.

"Mum, you said ..." he exploded.

She put her hand over his mouth.

"I know, sweetheart. I did plan to take you, but ..."

"You ARE taking me. Just last night, you said, 'Get a good sleep. We have a big day coming up.'"

"Stop!" she snapped and took a deep breath, huffing it out like the Big Bad Wolf. "Last night I faced facts. I cannot keep track of you and the movers at the same time. If you were there, I'd be worried sick. You could get lost or hurt or ..."

"Please, Mum," he begged. "I'll be good. I'll be an ANGEL! You promised ..."

But she had not promised and they both knew it.

"It wouldn't be fun for you anyway," she continued. "Hazel is coming to pick you up. You're going to sleep over at her house. You've never been on a sleepover like other kids, Birdie. Here's your chance. And tomorrow I'm coming back to get you."

"Kids don't have sleepovers at their babysitters," he said, but she swept on.

"I'll be back for you early tomorrow. We'll go to our new home together then."

"Tomorrow?" he cried, boomeranging around the room, missing the piled-up boxes by inches. When he fetched up in front of her again, she grabbed him and held on.

"You'll have fun at Hazel's," she insisted, almost shouting herself. Then, more quietly, "Birdie darling, be reasonable. Hazel will be here any minute and the movers are due in an hour. You have to get dressed!"

"I don't feel reasonable and I don't want to stay with a babysitter," he flung at her, pulling free. "I hate you!"

She looked stricken and he was glad. He backed away and stood stiffly, ready to do battle. Then he glimpsed the tears gathering on her eyelashes. He hated it when she cried. It wasn't fair.

He whirled and shot up the stairs.

If only his father had not taken off, this would not be happening. Mum was different before his dad walked out on them. She stayed home. Every afternoon when he came in from school, she was waiting with milk and homemade cookies or some other treat. She sat smiling at him, wanting to hear every detail of his day. She laughed more than she cried then. It had been great.

Well, mostly it had been great. Sometimes, when his day was downright boring, he had wished she would just leave him to watch TV. Sometimes the true answer to her question "What happened to my Bird today?" was "Nothing." Or, to be more truthful, "Nothing good." He had trouble staying still and paying attention. They had parent-teacher conferences. But when he got home, both of them pretended he was doing fine. And he always came up with some little triumph to tell her.

A couple of times, in desperation, he made up stuff. But that had backfired.

"The art teacher says I'm gifted," he told her once.

All the art teacher had ever said

to him was "Can't you keep still, young man?" But his mother almost phoned her to see if he should have extra art classes.

"I don't WANT art lessons," he pleaded.

"Leave him alone," his father said. "You don't want the big homecoming quiz every day, do you, Dick? You want her to treat you as though you can breathe all on your own."

This upset Mum so much that she forgot the art lessons.

Still Dickon hated it when his father spoke in that hard, joking voice. Somehow, he knew that Dad was really speaking to Mum, not to him. But Dad hadn't been home that much. He worked most afternoons and evenings. On weekends, he either watched the sports channel or slept. Mum made excuses for him at first.

"Your father is overtired and mustn't be bothered about us for a bit," she said.

But before long she gave up the little speeches about how exhausted Dad was. A few months later Dickon's father moved out.

Dickon was surprised at first by how little had changed. The days marched calmly by for a while. Yet that calm spell did not last. When Mum came to believe Dad was gone for good, she began to cry all the time. Dickon thought she might never stop. They moved in with Aunt Eloise for a while. Aunt Eloise's apartment was crammed with things he mustn't move, mustn't touch, mustn't break.

He smashed a porcelain figurine by mistake. Then his mother's doctor told her it was time she made a new life. So Mum found a part-time job and they moved back into the house they had lived in before the break-up. Dad had taken all his stuff and gone out west. He sent Dickon one postcard, but all it said was, "Sorry, son." His son threw it away before Mum saw it.

The townhouse echoed with emptiness after that.

"Where has he gone?" Dickon asked, bracing himself.

But she just said, "Calgary," in a dead voice. They left it at that.

In those days, she came in after he did and she was often too tired to cook. They ate meals out of boxes and there were no more homemade cookies. She promised that soon things would change.

Now she had a full-time job at the bank where she had worked before she was married. It was in Riverside, a town near Guelph. Because Monday was Canada Day, her new job began on Tuesday morning. She had landed the job because she was a whiz on the computer.

"That's one favor your father did me," she had told Dickon, "insisting I do the tax returns and family accounts and answer any E-mail we got. It made me mad sometimes, but I kept up my computer skills. They were impressed."

Dickon dug a shirt out of a box of clothes. He was about to put it on when he saw it had a little gorilla on it with a balloon coming out of its mouth saying, "Aren't I a cute kid?"

"Yuck," he grunted, shoving it out of sight. He hauled a plain blue one over his head and jammed his bare feet into his runners. Mum hated it when he didn't put on socks. Then he pounded down the stairs to the kitchen.

Mum was thrusting used bedding into a garbage bag. For a second, he thought she had forgotten him. Then she said, half under her breath, "After today, it will be as if we'd never lived in these rooms, Bird."

She fished out a Kleenex and blew her nose. He gave up the fight. He would stay at Hazel's, but he would not comfort his mother. He grabbed his backpack and made for the door.

"You mean you're all set?" Hazel said, grinning down at him as he nearly careened into her. "I'll bet you forgot your toothbrush."

"I did not," he told her, dodging past. "So long, Mum."

"Birdie, you have to clean those glasses," his mother called after him. "They're filthy."

Pretending not to hear, he sprinted to the car, clambered in and buckled the belt. Through the car window, he watched Hazel hugging his mother. Well, let her. She had not been counting on seeing the new house. His mother waved. He paused, but finally held his hand up in a stiff salute like the Queen.

Then they were off. As soon as they rounded the corner, Dickon relaxed. Hazel pulled into Jumbo Video and he chose three movies he knew his mother would not let him watch. Of all his babysitters, Hazel Henderson was the one he liked best because she did not try to make him keep all his mother's rules.

At Hazel's he shoved in the first video and settled down to watch.

Hazel slipped his glasses off his face and cleaned them on her shirt.

"Thanks," he muttered as he put them back on his nose. He was surprised at how much better he saw through clean lenses. He never noticed until he was reminded.

"You are entirely welcome," she said.

She went away and came back with a glass of juice and a peanut butter sandwich.

"Your mother said you had no breakfast," she said.

"Thanks," he said again, not looking at her.

She sat down to watch with him. The violence in the videos comforted him somehow. When he threw shadow punches at the tough guys on the screen, Hazel laughed and applauded. She thought he was cute. She said so and he clowned around, making her laugh even harder.

Mum would not have laughed. Mum would have switched off the set and talked to him about how much she wanted him to be a "gentle man." Not like his father was what she meant, he thought. After all, there was no chance he would turn out like one of the bad guys in the videos she hated. She must know that he just was not tough enough. If he only had been, the kids at school might have steered clear of him.

That night, he lay awake wondering if his mother had been sorry that she had left him behind. Probably not. She kept telling him, "You're all I have left." She never seemed to notice that she was all he had left too.

Shortly before eleven she came for him, a Cheshire cat smile pasted on her face. When her eyes were squinched up like that it always meant that her head ached.

"Come here, my son," she said, stretching out her arms. "I need a hug."

He let her hug him, but he didn't hug her back. Headache or no, she should have taken him with her. When he stepped back, he saw that she was hurt. He was sorry, but it was too late.

"Poor Julie," Hazel said, giving her a quick kiss that landed in the air next to her ear. "You look beat."

"Who me?" his mother said, rolling her eyes. The two women exchanged a grown-up look. He hated that.

"Let's GO, Mum," he urged, heading for the car. "You said today's the real moving day, remember?"

He ran around and opened her car door for her.

"I remember," Julie Fielding said, and her Cheshire cat smile warmed into a real grin. "And we're off, the two of us, into the wild blue yonder to make a fabulous fresh start on life."

As he slid into the car, he studied his mother. She did look tired. She was faking excitement for his sake, but her heart wasn't in it. She took a deep breath and burst into their theme song, "Side by Side." He joined in, changing the words.

"We ain't got a nickel for spending ..."

He hesitated and she made up the next line.

"And the world we are used to is ending. But we'll make it through..."

"Just me and you," he added happily.

"Side by side," they finished together.

"Oh, Birdie, you are such a comfort," she said.

"I know it," he told her. "Now step on the gas, Mum. I want my fresh start to start!"

On the Way

"I have to stop by the pharmacy," Mum said, "to get your pills and something for me."

"Headache pills," he said, wanting her to know that he was as smart as Hazel.

"How do you know my head aches?" she said.

"Psychic," he shot back, grinning.

She parked in front of the drugstore and got out. Then she paused, peering in at him.

"Promise me you will not stir from this car," she said.

"I promise," he said, sounding as bored as he could.

She sped away. Dickon reached out to turn on the car radio, but his mother had the keys. He pulled off his glasses, folded them up and shoved them into the glove compartment. He yanked off his runners and wiggled his toes inside his striped socks. He bunched them up, stretched them wide apart and spoke kindly to them.

"Want a fresh start, toes?" he asked.

His toes were too hot to chat. They drooped. He stripped off the socks and put his hot, sweaty feet on the dashboard to air. His toes liked that. They frisked like excited tadpoles.

His mother was taking FOREVER.

Then he saw a lady walking her dog. Snapping open the glove compartment, he fished out his glasses for a better look. How he longed for a dog of his very own! He'd never get one if his mother had any say in the matter.

"A dog attacked me when I was three," she said whenever the subject came up. Dickon had seen the tiny scar on her little finger where the dog had nipped her. She still shuddered at the memory of the brute beast.

But that was silly. His mother had not been three for a long, long time, and he had much bigger scars. He had a huge one on his leg from catching it on a nail when he was climbing a fence. He was not afraid of nails. Or fences.

The lady was walking an Old English sheepdog puppy. It bounced and bumbled around her feet, almost tripping her. She was laughing out loud. He opened the door a crack to listen.

"Stop it, Ebeneezer, you daft creature," he heard her say.

The puppy sat down with a bump and gazed up at her, his head cocked a little on one side. He looked more cuddly than a stuffed toy. Then he bounced up and romped ahead, tugging his mistress along. When they passed close by, Dickon longed to jump out and ask to pat Ebeneezer. He opened the door wider. It would only take five seconds.

With one bare foot halfway out, he remembered his promise. His moment of happiness blew away like a helium balloon. Glowering, he pulled his foot back in and shut the car door.

Then he spotted Jim and Jason Bridgeman across the street and his mother coming back from the pharmacy. He ducked down. What if Jim yelled, "Hiya, Dizzy Dick," or "What's new, Twitchy?"?

Dickon had never told his mother about the teasing. Now they were moving away. If Jim didn't spot him, she need never know.

Twitch. Spacey. Dizzy Dick. Boy Jerky. Jim's jeers sounded again inside Dickon's head as he crouched low, keeping his head turned to hide his face. The names were as hard to brush aside as black flies in June. They stung like fly bites too.

The teacher had called him Mr. Fidget

twice, but the twins hadn't heard. When she brought a jumping bean home from a trip to Mexico, though, Jim had called him Beano for days.

"Here I am at last," his mother said, sliding in next to him. "That store is so crowded. Are you all right, Bird?"

"Sure. Are we leaving now?" he asked, twisting to see if the boys were out of sight. Tension sharpened his voice.

"We are leaving this minute," she said. "Please, Birdie, forgive me for yesterday and cheer up. Today should be fun."

Her hand, reaching to insert the ignition key, shook. He scowled. She made such a big deal out of everything. His glasses had slipped down. He shoved them back so fiercely that the nosepiece dug into him. She was waiting for an apology. If he didn't give it, she'd start in at him again. Just in time, he muttered, "Sorry."

She swallowed and said, "Me too. Are you hungry?"

"Nope," he said.

Once he had taken his medication,

he wouldn't be hungry for hours. Then, all of a sudden, he'd be ravenous. Why didn't she remember?

"Okay. Forget I mentioned it," she said in her Poor Me voice.

As the car merged with the highway traffic, it dawned on him that she might be hungry even if he were not. Feeling ashamed, he bent and put his shoes back on without any socks. Before she could notice, he kicked the socks under the seat. She'd like him to tell her, "You ought to eat something. Go ahead and stop," but the words stuck in his throat. She was the grown-up, not him.

"Are you excited, Bird?" she asked, trying once again to make the day a glad one.

"Yeah," he said. "I mean, sure."

Maybe he really was excited. After all, the two of them were getting away from the city where Dad had left them. Nobody knew anything about them in Riverside. The people at the bank knew his mother, but his father had never once been there.

Even more important, he would never again have to watch out for the Bridgeman brothers. The kids in the new place had not known him before he started taking his pills. Maybe they wouldn't throw names at him. Before he got the medication, he had been a bit hyper. He still was sometimes. He kind of liked it once in a while, going wild and screeching and bouncing off the furniture.

"Wired," the doctor called it.

"Off the wall," his mother said.

"Zoo boy," the girl next door had said once.

"Just being an active child," his dad had said, but he had been wrong. Gregory in his class was an active boy, good at sports, a born sprinter. He, Dickon, was hyperactive. The doctor had said so.

"How far is it now?" he burst out, the words exploding out of him like corn popping. "How far? How long? When will we be there? What's the house like? Is my room big?"

"Settle down, Birdie," she said, her voice tired but half-laughing. "You sound like a cap gun. I've told you all that stuff. Quit winding yourself up."

Probably she had told him. He half-knew bits and pieces but he needed to hear it all more than once. Why couldn't she just tell him?

Drumming his fingertips on the edge of the window, he peered out at the busy highway.

"Can you get me some Kleenex out of my purse?" she asked.

He reached back, swung her bag up off the floor, found a little package of tissues and handed it over. Then he dropped the unzipped purse back with a thud.

His mother blew her nose. Then she answered his questions, all but one.

"You didn't say what the house is like," he prompted when she stopped speaking.

"Wait and see," she told him. "It won't be long now. Remember, even if it isn't a palace, it is ours. It was the only place I could find for the money I had that was all ready to move into. I am no good at fixing things."

Dad could fix anything. Both of them thought of him, but neither said so.

Dickon put his glasses in their case and slumped down, letting his eyelids plop shut. Quietly, so she wouldn't notice, he dug his knuckles into his closed eyes and watched the colors swirl and float and pinwheel around like those in his old kaleidoscope. Blue, purple, flashes of green, bursts of yellow. He loved the whirling rainbow colors. They were so much brighter, more vivid, than anything in his real world. They soothed him, smoothing down the spikes of prickly tension.

"Stop that, Birdie," she said.

Why? What harm was it doing her? Glowering, he muttered, "Okay. Wake me up when we get there."

It seemed only seconds before she called him.

"Nearly there, Birdie," she said.

He sat up and stared out the car windows. They were creeping along one of the most boring streets he had ever seen. They passed a street sign that said Applewood Road. His mother turned into another street as dull as the first. Orchard Drive. Dickon looked for fruit trees but saw only a row of spindly maple saplings, one in front of each house.

"Where ... ?" he began.

Before he could finish, she stopped in front of a house. It was one in a long row of houses identical except for their color: brown, gray, slate-colored, brown ... His mother had parked in front of a gray one.

Hope, which had been so bright inside him, faded. That wasn't a home. It was a box.

"Put on your glasses," his mother urged. "It's not that bad. And it's our very own. We even have a tree."

Dickon dug out his glasses case once again and put on the spectacles. Then he peered through them. The house looked even worse. He strained to keep his face blank and forced his lips to smile.

But she was not fooled.

"You hate it," she said flatly.

"I haven't seen inside yet," he said

loudly, doing his best to meet her searching gaze. "I was expecting something ... different, that's all."

She had gotten out of the car and now she just stood there, staring at the house, not answering.

He climbed out and tried for a better smile.

"Let's have the Tour, lady," he said. "I never judge a house by its ... its front door."

"Follow me," she said, starting up the three gray steps to the door. "You'll at least have your own room."

Dickon did not remind her that he had always had his own room. He fell in behind her. Then a strange voice said, "Hello, Mrs. Fielding. Welcome to Orchard Drive. You must be Dick."

"That's the Humane Society ..."

Julie Fielding turned to the next-door neighbor who had come out to welcome them.

"Oh, hello, Mrs. Nelson. Please, call me Julie," she said. "Yes, this is my son. He's Dickon, not Dick. I'm about to give him his first tour of our new home."

"You call me Amy. I won't hold you up then. Hi, Dickon. I don't think I've ever heard that name before."

She had short fat curls all over her head that bobbed as she moved. Her face was rosy and she had a warm smile. Her dress was covered with pink flowers and she wore a pink apron. Even her glasses, which were hung on a chain around her neck, had pink frames.

"I named him after Dickon in *The Secret Garden*, the boy who charms the animals," Dickon's mother said.

"I'm not much of a reader," Mrs. Nelson said, "but my granddaughter has the video. I watched some when I was babysitting. Wasn't Dickon the one with the lamb?"

"Yes," Julie Fielding said. "But you really should read the story."

Dickon grinned. His father had called *The Secret Garden* "Julie's Bible." Dad usually called him Dick, which made Mum mad because it made people think that his long name was Richard. She had started calling him Dickybird when he was too little to make a fuss. He had not paid attention until his parents began squabbling over it.

"Julie, stop. It's as bad as calling the boy Tweetie," Dad had yelled once.

Not long after that, she had shortened it to Bird or Birdie. He had been about to tell her he wanted to be called Dickon when Dad had left and it was too late.

Like it or not, he was Birdie for now. But someday, he would be Dickon. Maybe it would happen here in this new place. Maybe it would be part of the fresh start.

He wished he could be like Dickon Sowerby in *The Secret Garden*. That boy had all the pets he wanted. And he was so free! If he had wanted a dog ...

"I don't have a pet lamb," their new neighbor said, smiling, "but I do have a pet. You'll have to come over and meet Charlie after you've had the tour."

Mum waved goodbye to Mrs. Nelson and beckoned Dickon into the house. He took a last look at the outside as he started up the steps. On either side of the door was a narrow window. The roof had a little slant, but he saw at once that there was no upstairs. It reminded him of the houses he had drawn in kindergarten before he had learned to make the roof go up to a point and add a fat chimney. There was no chimney here. Santa Claus would be left out in the cold.

"Right this way, Mr. Fielding," his mother was saying.

Dickon marched in like a soldier ordered into battle, hoping against hope that there would be something for him to rave about. She wanted him to be pleased. If there was not one single good thing, what would he do?

The front hall was a small, square space, almost too tiny to hold the two of them. He peered through the two doors opening out of it on either side. The living room was on the right and the kitchen on the left. The bathroom was straight ahead of him and there were two bedrooms, one on either side of the bathroom. Stacks of boxes and a couple of bulging garbage bags blocked their way. That was all.

"We'll eat in the kitchen," she said. "It's cozy, isn't it?"

"Yeah," he lied. "I like eating in the kitchen."

Cramped was a better word

And ever since Dad had gone, the two of them had eaten in front of the TV.

"That's your room," she said, pointing.

Her voice shook. She'd fall apart in ten seconds if he didn't snap out of this gloom. He came to life with a jerk and lurched forward, squeezing past all the boxes, into his new room. His bed, his huge box of Lego and his bookcase almost filled the narrow space. His desk was jammed behind the door with his chair upside-down on top of it.

Oh, no! She had hung his old teddy bear curtains in the windows! She'd probably brought his teddy bear mug too.

"It's cool," he bellowed. "I like it a lot. Honestly, Mum. I think it's great."

"No, you don't," his mother answered, squeezing past him. "It's too small and it only has one little window and the walls are lima bean green. I hate it too. But my walls are eggplant purple." She sank onto the bed and gave a small smile. "We won't be here forever, Bird. Just until I find a job that pays a bit more. We can make a new start here, though. As soon as I get some free time, I'll paint your bedroom."

"But I do like it. I do. Really," he insisted, crashing across to the window. "Look at my view."

He shouldn't have said that before he checked.

The squinchy little backyard ended in a chain link fence. On the far side was a large building and a huge grassy fenced-in area. What was it? It could be a baseball diamond almost, but he couldn't see any bases. There were no trees either.

"That's the Humane Society," his mother told him. "They said we would hardly hear the barking, but I'm not so sure. The cages have runs on the other side, but they may well exercise the animals inside that fenced-in field."

The Humane Society! Dogs!

Long ago, when Dickon was four, Dad had brought home a puppy from the Humane Society. Dickon still remembered that puppy even though his mother had been so upset that his father had taken it back an hour later. Maybe being so close to lots of dogs would change her mind about them. Then, at last, he would get a pup all his own.

"It is superb, excellent, Mum!" he shouted, putting on a maniac act. "It's my dream house!"

He whirled to hug her. She hated the house as much as he did. But they were getting a fresh start. She had said so. And, all at once, a real grin spread across his face for the first time since she had left him behind the day before.

Her big gray eyes filled with tears. She hugged him back. One tear plopped down behind his ear and made him jump.

"You should go next door for that cup of tea," he told her, wiggling free. "I'll stay and unpack my stuff."

"Oh, Birdie, you should come too," she said.

He knew how to change her mind.

He shot away from her, leaped onto his bed and began to bounce. He had been cooped up in the car so long that he felt as fizzy as a shaken pop can. He could not sit and sip lemonade like a good boy.

Wham, wham, wham!

"Oh, baby, do calm down," she begged.

He thudded to the floor and glanced through his window. Two women were coming out of the building and walking up the street that ran along the end of the block. Did they work at the Humane Society? He stared at them, taking in every detail of their appearance. One was black and extra tall with short curly hair. She had on jeans and a denim shirt and she took long steps so the other one had to trot to keep up. The smaller woman only came up to the tall one's jaw, and her hair, which was long and shoved behind her ears, was so fair it was nearly white. She turned to speak to the other one and her white teeth flashed.

Then they paused and looked up at a sign attached to the fence. He could not see the words, of course, but he was curious. He would have to drag Mum out on a detective walk.

His mother looked to see what had caught his attention.

"I wonder who those two are," she said idly, "and what that sign says. *NO DOGS ALLOWED* would be nice."

"No, it wouldn't. If I had a dog ..." he began in spite of himself

"Now, Birdie, you know it isn't possible," Julie Fielding said, heaving a sigh. "I wish they were not right in our backyard. That had better be a good stout fence. At least you can't get through it."

"Yeah, yeah," Dickon said.

If he didn't get a dog before he grew up, he would have one then for sure. Suddenly, the idea of being this close to the Humane Society made him so excited that he spun in a circle with his arms stretched wide. His mother leaned out of the way.

"All right," she said weakly. "I'll go. I have a few questions to ask. But I'll take my cell phone."

"Fresh start," he hummed to himself once the door closed. "Fresh start, fresh start. Dogs, dogs, DOGS!"

Maybe, like Mary in *The Secret Garden*, he would find magic on the other side of the fence.

Kids and Dogs

After supper, Dickon coaxed his mother out for a walk. He wanted to see that sign.

"Wait up, Mum," he said when they had reached it. "I have a stone in my shoe."

He hopped on one foot while he read. It was not easy. She waited, never guessing what he was up to.

DOG CARE PLUS OBEDIENCE TRAINING
July 2 – July 26
Children 10 to 14
Weekday Afternoons 1:00 to 3:30 p.m.
Learn to train, groom and care for your dog.
Snacks provided for kids and dogs.

The class began on Tuesday!

"Have you got it out?" his mother asked.

He stared at her blankly. Then he remembered the phantom stone in his shoe.

"Yup," he said and walked on, dreaming of dogs.

His mother studied his face.

"You are to stay on our property, remember," Julie Fielding reminded her son sternly.

"Okay, okay," he said.

"You'll miss your friends, but you can make new ones when school starts," she put in.

Friends? That was a good one.

Well, he reminded himself, here nobody knows I'm weird. They haven't heard the Bridgemans calling me names.

If the kids here start, at least they'll be different ones. I won't let them hear Mum calling me Birdie, not if I can help it.

"Home again, home again," she said in a cheery voice.

"Jiggety-jig," he said, heading into his room.

"You need a bath, Birdie," she called after him.

"I'm Birdie for now," he muttered, "but I won't be Birdie forever. Even Mum can't call a grown-up man 'Birdie.'"

The next day was Canada Day. Dad had taken them to a great fireworks display two years ago. Last summer, neither of them had even noticed Canada Day. This year was going to be another Non Canada Day, Birdie was sure.

He was watching TV when Mum groaned.

"What's wrong?" he asked, not really interested.

"They are going to be running a dog training school of some kind right behind this house," she said. "Oh, dear. You'll have to keep away from that."

Hadn't she read the sign He jumped up and ran to look over her shoulder. There was a picture of the tall woman, smiling. She was holding a dog in her arms.

LESLIE HAWKIN TEACHES DOGS MANNERS, the headline read.

"Read out what it says," he urged.

Leslie Hawkin, Mum read, from the Riverside Humane Society, was running a summer program for children whose dogs needed to learn some manners. Basic Dog Obedience would be taught, plus tips on grooming and general care for a pet.

"They will learn to brush their dogs' teeth," she read.

"She must be crazy," his mother said with a shudder. "When the kids get bitten, she'll be sued pronto."

Dickon opened his mouth to argue and then knew he should let her forget. But he was so excited that he had to go to his room so she would not guess.

The two of them spent all day Monday unpacking boxes and putting things in new places. If only Tuesday would hurry up and come!

His mother left him a list of instructions when she went to work the next morning. His food was all prepared. He would not even have to make himself a piece of toast. Her cell phone number was written up everywhere. She had set an alarm to ring every hour. When he heard it, he was to check in with Mrs. Nelson. At least he didn't have to go over and spend the day with her. Neither he nor the neighbor lady had liked that idea.

He watched TV all morning. When the programs got too babyish, he began building a Lego wall across his bedroom door. It left room at the side for him to get in, but it let him leave his door open without his mother seeing out the window. She would see his Lego wall instead with its windows and doors, steps and terraces. He was good at Lego when he could do whatever he liked with it.

He took breaks, checking his window view and calling the lady next door whenever the alarm went off. She told him all about Charlie, who turned out to be her pet hedgehog. He went over to see Charlie and was astounded by the tiny animal who, when he rolled himself up, was about the size of a tennis ball.

After Dickon ate half his sandwich and drank his first glass of milk, he settled down cross-legged on his bed and gazed out at the Humane Society yard. Nothing was happening. But he stayed put, watching. His teachers would have been amazed.

"If you'd stop fidgeting and concentrate instead," Mrs. Abcock had said to him in front of them all, "you might make some progress, Dick. You need to pull up your socks or you'll spend your entire life in Grade Two."

He looked at his feet. No socks to pull up. And he was out of Grade Two, maybe even going into Grade Four. Mum had not got his school class settled yet.

Where were the dog-training kids?

He stared at his digital watch. It was time. His feet jiggled up and down, up and down, but his eyes never shifted from the windowpane.

Finally, the tall lady he had seen two days before arrived. She set up a card table and put out some papers. Then she, too, waited. At last, a car pulled up and two kids, two dogs and a parent got out. They disappeared into the building. Then the girls came out to the field, leaving the adult inside to register and pay, Dickon supposed.

"Over here, girls," Leslie Hawkin called to them.

Good. He could hear every word. Wrestling the window wide open had been worth it.

"I'm Leslie Hawkin," she said. "Now who are you two?"

One girl looked wild and the other tame. The wild one had black curly hair that looked as though it would defeat the toughest brush. Her skin was a warm brown and her shorts were a blinding orange. Her T-shirt had sunflowers all over it. A dog — part terrier, part something else — bounced around her, almost knocking her off her feet.

The tame girl was shorter with long brown hair. She had pink cheeks and wore white shorts, a pale pink T-shirt and glasses. They both had runners on, but the wild girl had no socks and the tame one's socks just matched her shirt. Her dog was a tiny Manchester terrier.

"I'm Kristin Shortreed," she said. "I'm eleven."

"Almost eleven. Her birthday's next Friday," the wild one put in. "I'm Jody Parr and I've been eleven for a month."

Their dogs were prancing around like cartoon animals. Leslie frowned.

"Cut it out, Poppet. Settle down," Jody yelled at her pup. "Sit. I said SIT!"

"She won't, Jody," the other girl told her in a prissy voice. "Watch Hercules. Sit, Hercules."

Hercules sat for a split second. Then he sprang up and jumped to lick her hand. His giant name was a joke.

Dickon started to laugh but hushed

so he could hear more.

"So he sits. So what? You can't make him stay sitting, Kristin, can you? Admit it. And he never comes when he's called," Jody said, shoving hard on Poppet's rump. "Poppet almost always comes."

"Enough already," said the teacher. "I need to make a list of your names, your dogs' names and where I can reach you."

Others were coming outside. A thirteen-year-old boy called Trevor with a golden retriever had arrived while they were arguing. His dog's name was Taffy.

"If they did what we told them, we wouldn't be here," he said as the girls started up their argument again. "My mum says if Taffy doesn't smarten up, she's going to give her to my cousins in the country."

"Aw, Trevor, that's awful," Kristin said. "My mum gets mad at Hercules, but really she likes him better than she likes us kids. He trails after her all day, and whenever she sits down, he's up on her lap in one flying leap."

Other children came. They had to open and shut a gate to get into the fenced-in area. It wasn't so simple with their dogs bouncing around their feet. Every single kid had a dog on a leash. Some were half-grown puppies, but some looked adult. One was humungous! A couple of the others were big, but not like that one.

Not one was well behaved. They pulled ahead or dragged behind, scratched themselves, jumped up on people or tried to pick fights.

Dickon ran into the kitchen and took down his mother's birdwatching binoculars. She had not yet used them here, but she had hung them carefully on a hook by the kitchen window.

"This," he murmured, raising them to his eyes, "is a special occasion."

Every face sprang up, clear and sharp, before him. He could lip-read much better.

Two new girls appeared. Sylvia had a dog called Pippin. Dickon did not know what breed it was, but he liked it.

"My dog is named Brisbane," said

the other girl. "And I'm Maria Sanchez."

Brisbane was a chunky yellow Lab. Maria's hair hung in long, skinny braids and her smile was wide.

Taffy began running around Trevor's legs in circles, and all at once she dashed over to sniff Jody's dog. The boy's knees buckled and a friendly free-for-all broke out.

Leslie Hawkin jumped up and sorted out dogs and owners, calling every sinner by name. The animals, even the monster whose name was Tallboy, hung their heads like children caught with their hands in the cookie jar.

Dickon shook with silent laughter. Twice he put down the binoculars and jigged up and down in excitement. Two more children arrived, Jake Chang with a Boston bull terrier and Chico whose last name Dickon did not catch. He had a beautiful German shepherd named Fancy.

Last of all came a smallish girl with a big frown on her face. Her dog seemed better behaved than most, but Dickon could tell he was longing to bounce higher than any of them.

"And whom have we here?" Leslie asked, smiling.

The girl stood straight as a soldier. Just before she spoke, Dickon guessed her secret. She was sure nobody would like her. He knew how that felt. But why was she so certain she would be an outsider?

"I'm Jenny English," she said in a very English voice. "And my dog's name is Copperkins, but I call him Perkins. He's a soft-coated Wheaton terrier. He's my birthday present. We got him a month ago, just after we moved here from London. I'm twelve."

"He's lovely, Jenny," Leslie said, smiling at her. "He looks so well cared for. And happy."

"Yes," the girl said. Then she ducked her head and muttered, "We took him to the groomer yesterday."

"He's neat," Jody said, grinning at her. "When mine comes home from the groomer, he still looks like a floor mop."

"Pippin is supposed to be part Wheaton," Sylvia said. "I got her from the Humane Society in Toronto."

Dickon lost sight of them in the crowd then, but not before he saw Jenny give Pippin a measuring look. Jody grinned at her again. And just before Daniel cut off his view he saw Jenny relax a bit and smile shyly back at the wild girl.

Then the teacher walked into the field and blew a loud blast on a whistle. All the dogs, big and small, cocked their heads at the sharp sound.

"Pay attention, everyone. The first class is now starting. Get your dogs and back up until you are spread out in a big circle. Shorten those leashes until the animals cannot get close to each other. Trevor, give Taffy a sharp jerk and tell her 'NO!'"

Trevor jerked on the leash and Taffy wagged her tail happily. She was not going to obey him.

Dickon leaned forward so far that he slid onto the floor, landing with a flump. He kept his hold on the binoculars somehow. Sighing with relief, he picked himself up.

He climbed onto the bed again and went on watching. His body ached to bounce up and down a few times. His mattress was great for bouncing. But if he did, he might miss something.

Another boy came racing around the building, letting the gate clang shut behind him. His dog was a tri-colored, lop-eared collie. The boy was breathless and red in the face, but the collie looked calm and dignified.

"Hi, Ruff," Jody called. "Hi, Andy." Ruff looked down her noble nose as though the others were mere babies and she was the only adult.

"Sorry I'm late. I'm Anthony Blake," the newcomer said. "I got held up ..."

"After today, I want you all here on time," the teacher announced. "We must concentrate if we want to make a difference in four weeks. Latecomers will distract the dogs. We'll have a break at two-thirty. We can chat then."

The children were in their circle now. The huge dog was lying down and Daniel, his master, was doing his best to yank him up again. Leslie walked over. Dickon missed seeing what she did, but all at once the gangling dog was sitting up with a startled look on his face.

"You have to be firm, Daniel. Tallboy won't understand sweet talk. You have to show him you mean business."

"Yes, Leslie, I know. But he just ..."

"No excuses. If you aren't ready to learn, take Tallboy and go on home," Leslie said. "He's big, of course, but you are smarter and he is wearing a choke chain. He's young, too, and has not been taught bad habits."

She returned to her spot. The whistle blew another sharp blast.

Dickon set the heavy binoculars down on the windowsill and shook his fingers.

"Today we won't have time for a whole class," Leslie said. "I just want to meet you all and check that you have choke chain collars for your dogs."

"I don't want to choke Hercules," Kristin protested. "He's so little and he shouldn't be hurt."

"Me neither," murmured Maria.

Leslie went over and put a choke collar on Kristin's arm.

"If you put it on properly, it won't really choke your dog. It'll just get his attention. Then you loosen your tug. Like this."

She jerked the leash. Kristin's mouth opened. Before she could speak, the leash fell slack.

"Oh," she said, looking down at her arm. There was no mark.

Dickon especially liked Kristin and Jody. Kristin looked calm and friendly, and Jody seemed exciting. Friendly too, but differently. He liked Jenny too. He could tell she was feeling shy. He saw Jody speak to her. She must have made a joke. Jenny glanced nervously at Leslie and then smiled back.

Dickon's throat ached with his yearning to run out and leap into the ring of kids with a dog of his very own. He would instantly belong. It wouldn't matter that the others were older and taller. Everybody in the world was bigger than Birdie Fielding. Except Jenny maybe.

A shriek made Dickon snap to attention.

Taffy had pulled loose and was

running away. Dickon looked to where she was heading and saw the hole in the fence. It was low and not huge, but a dog could wriggle through it. And it led right into Dickon's yard.

"Gotcha!" Trevor caught hold of his dog's tail. Taffy sat down and allowed him to pick up her leash.

Twenty minutes later, all the children were handed juice boxes and the dogs were given water. Then, in no time at all, it was over. Everyone left. Dickon, watching them go, was making a plan.

Tomorrow, before the kids came, he would wiggle through the hole in the fence. He was sure that he would fit. Then he would hang around, at the edge, quiet and interested. He would not fidget or yell. He would take his pill last thing. He'd be a shadow of a boy. If he did it just right, Leslie Hawkin had to let him stay. Jody would take his part for sure. He curled up and began a daydream in which he got a dog, a beautiful big one with brown eyes filled with love. His dog was obedient right away.

"I'm Dickon Bird"

The slam of a car door woke him. He leaped up and zoomed into the hall.

"Hi, Mum," he said, suddenly pleased to see her.

"Hi yourself, my sweet Birdie," she said, dumping groceries onto the kitchen table and hugging him. "Did you think I was never coming?"

"No," he said, surprised. Then he

stole a look at his watch. Five-forty-five. She had said she would be home by five at the latest.

"I knew you'd call if something was wrong," he said.

He was in luck. She was so taken up with her first full day at her new job that she forgot to quiz him about what he'd done all day.

"So what's new, Chickabid?" she asked finally through a yawn.

He told her he'd watched TV and had lunch and worked on his Lego.

"Kids came to a dog class at the Humane Society," he threw in, casually.

"Oh, baby, they want me to work late for the first two weeks," she burst out, not hearing what he said. She launched into the story of her day. It sounded dull to him, but clearly she had found it a great challenge.

"Wow," he murmured, realizing she had paused for him to react. "Wow" should be safe.

At last she got up and started making their supper.

They had almost finished eating before Dickon realized that his mother was feeling guilty because she was going to be late coming home for a while.

"Don't worry," he said, keeping his voice steady, hiding his relief.

"But I hate leaving you alone," she began.

"I'll be fine," he said, slugging down the milk she had poured. "I was okay today, wasn't I?"

"It might be against the law," she said. "I'll ask Mrs. Nelson to watch out for you. And I'll check in at noon. You're pretty sensible."

"I'm TOTALLY sensible," he said.

A dog barked shrilly. Another answered. His mother frowned.

"I wish we were not so close to that place," she said. "If one of those strays got loose and attacked you ..."

"Really, Mum, you've been watching too much violent TV," he teased.

His voice must have sounded funny. She stared at him. He shifted his feet and balled his hands into fists. If only something would distract her!

The phone rang.

What a relief! She was soon chattering with someone from work. He parked himself in front of the TV. Although she always said he watched too much television, he knew she relaxed when she heard it go on. After all, her darling was safe in front of the tube. Ha!

Wednesday morning crawled by. He visited Mrs. Nelson and Charlie. She was giving the tiny hedgehog a bath in the basin. Dickon watched in fascination.

Charlie kept trying to escape. As she scrambled up the enamel sides of the basin and slipped back, her underside grew beautifully clean. Mrs. Nelson laughed gently at her, but Dickon could see she was sympathetic.

By noon, he was at home waiting for his mother's check-up call. But she did not phone until after twelve-thirty. Then she chatted.

So he was later than he planned.

He slipped across the patch of grass that was his own yard and inspected the hole under the fence. The gap was big enough. Without taking time to look around, Dickon flung himself flat, prized up the wire and rolled under as far as he could. The left leg of his jeans snagged on a bit of metal. He pulled the denim loose and tried again. Wow! He had done it. Then feet thudded across the grass.

"Well, well, Kris, what have we here?" Jody's voice said from right above him.

Dickon blushed scarlet. Where had she come from? A dog's nose poked against his cheek. He rolled over and sat up.

Kristin giggled. "No, Hercules. Don't eat him alive."

"It's an alien," Jody said. "Hey, kid, what's your name?"

He was rattled.

"Birdie ..." he started. Then, trying to fix it, he got out, "I mean, Dickon."

"Why did you say 'Bird'?" Jody asked.

Dickon thought fast. "It's my last name. I'm Dickon Bird," he said.

Nobody would believe that. His ears burned.

"Dickon Bird. How cute," Jody said,

letting his blush pass.

Dickon opened his mouth and shut it again. The girls were introducing him to Poppet and Hercules. Other kids were coming over. Somehow the words he meant to say did not come out. Why were they all here early? He looked at his watch. One-thirty. They weren't early at all.

Then it dawned on him that if they did not know his real name they couldn't tell his mother he had been over here. Maybe it was safer to go on being Dickon Bird.

"All right, class," Leslie Hawkin called. "Time to start. Who, pray tell, might you be, young man?"

"His name's Dickon Bird," Kristin said with a small snort of laughter.

"Could I watch?" Dickon began, doing his best to appear responsible and quiet.

"I'm sorry but we don't let anyone watch who isn't signed up," the teacher said briskly. "You would be distracting to the dogs."

"I wouldn't," Dickon burst out. "Please, let me. I wouldn't ..."

"Run along home," she said sharply. No touch of warmth sounded in her voice now. "The class is too large as it is, and I've already told you ..."

At that exact moment a newcomer burst upon the scene.

Andy had left the gate open. A small black-and-white dog came flying through the space. One minute she was not there and the next she had dashed in among them, her dangling leash sailing through the air after her.

She was half Poppet's size. She might be no bigger than Hercules, but she had a silky coat that rippled in the breeze. She had a black patch over each eye with a white part coming down between. And she had incredible ears. They were black, too, and tall, shaped like butterfly wings. Her feathery tail curled up over her back one minute, streamed out behind her the next and, finally, tucked itself out of sight between her legs. To Dickon, that tail shouted, "I want to be friends ... I'm running away ... I'm afraid." He understood the little dog completely.

"Hello," he whispered and dropped down on one knee.

His words drew her. Her small, dainty face lifted and her pleading eyes looked right into his. Perhaps she chose him because he was the only child without a dog. In any case, she ran straight into his arms and cowered against him, whimpering.

"Who on earth ...?" Leslie started.

Then, a man shaped like an armored truck came charging around the building, bellowing, "Get back here, you birdbrain. NOW!"

Dickon stiffened, glaring, but the man did not notice.

"Catch that mutt," he roared. "Blast her, she's nothing but trouble."

Dickon's arms tightened around the small creature. He rose with her in his arms, the leash dangling. Then he stood still, not speaking to the man but whispering comforting words to the frightened dog he held.

"Easy, girl," he said in a shaking voice. "Don't be scared."

Her huge, feathery ears brushed his

cheek. They were the softest things he had ever felt. Like the butterfly kisses his mother used to give him with her eyelashes. The dog's golden brown eyes begged him for help.

He wanted to promise to keep her safe forever. But the man fetched up next to them, panting heavily. His cheeks were brick red. His eyes blazed. He bent over with a grunt and grabbed the leash. Then he stood, catching his breath and glaring at everyone.

"Don't ..." Dickon began.

Instantly, the man began to shout at the frightened dog.

"This is it for you," he told her. "No more peeing on the carpet, no more chewing shoes, no more running away when you are called. I've had enough. We are turning you in and if they have any brains you'll be dead before the day is out. Put her down again, boy. The little beast snaps."

The children had gathered, wide-eyed, in a ring around Dickon and the dog. But the man's rage frightened them almost as much as it scared the dog.

Everyone but Jody, the teacher and Dickon himself retreated to a safe distance.

Dickon's insides squeezed tight just as they had when his father had yelled at him or at his mother. In those days, he had run and left Mum to protect him. But now he must stand his ground. The little dog had run to him.

"Don't yell so loud." His words came out in a squeak, but they did come out. "You're scaring her."

"I'll yell at her if I please," the man snarled. "Put her down, I said. What happens to her is not your business. She deserves whatever she gets. She made a puddle of pee on my newspaper this morning before I had a chance to read the sports page. And she chewed up my girl's new Barbie."

Dickon had no choice. He set the dog on the ground as gently as he could. The man wheeled about and set out for the Humane Society building. As he did so, he jerked hard on the leash, tumbling the dog off her feet. Then, without glancing back, he dragged her

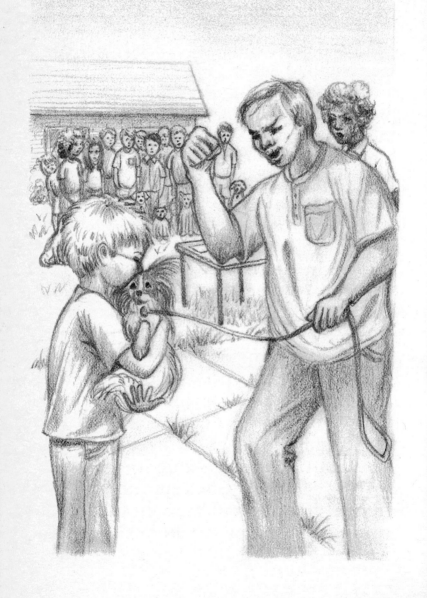

after him as though she were a pull toy, never giving her a chance to get her balance.

"Just a minute, mister!" Leslie shouted after him.

When he kept going, she strode to catch up. All the kids knew she was mad as a wet hen. They grinned.

"You fix him, Leslie," Travis said. But he kept his voice down.

"You're a BEAST!" Jody shouted after the striding man. Her voice shook, but it was at full volume.

The man charged on. Dickon agreed with Jody, but yelling would not help the dog. He ran after the pair, trying to think of how he could rescue her.

"What's her name?" he called in a desperate bid to slow the man down.

The man slowed slightly and stared at the boy dashing after him. Leslie turned too.

"What's it to you?" he snarled. Then he surprised Dickon by answering. "I'll tell you. It's a dumb name, but she's a dumb dog. Birdie! Her name's Birdie."

"Nothing You Can Do"

Dickon was so startled that he missed his footing and almost fell flat. Leslie grabbed his elbow and steadied him. They ran on.

Birdie! Had the man really said her name was Birdie?

"Bertie?" he called. "Did you say ..."

"I said Birdie. It ought to be Birdbrain, but it's Birdie."

"That's enough," Leslie's voice cut in,

silencing the man briefly.

Dickon's thoughts whirled.

She couldn't be Birdie. He was Birdie.

Birdie for now, he reminded himself. I'm really Dickon. I'm not Birdie at all.

The man had been forced to stop at the door. A family that had just found its lost calico cat was coming out, all smiles. They clustered together in the doorway, crooning over her. "Oh, Motley," the little girl said, "I thought you were dead."

The man tapped his foot. Then he looked at Dickon.

"My girl Tiffany named her. When she ran, her ears stuck out like wings or some stupid thing. But even Tiff agrees now she's really Birdbrain. Would you people move it? I have things to do."

The family ignored him, but they were soon gone. The door of the Humane Society swung shut behind the man, the dog and Leslie, who followed him in.

Dickon stared at the door. The other children crowded around, but only Jenny saw how pale he had grown.

"Are you all right?" she asked, moving close enough to touch him. "You look sick."

Dickon hardly heard her. Birdie. Her name was Birdie. It must mean something, but he felt too shocked to think clearly.

Through an open window, they could all hear the man inside raving on about how bad the dog was.

"I got her for my girl from a guy I know who works in a pet store. He said she was a purebred Papillon some woman had had for six months and then she had to go to England or someplace so she'd asked him what to do. He let me have her cheap. I should have known she wasn't worth fifty bucks."

"Purebred Papillons cost far more than fifty dollars," Leslie told him coldly. "They are still thought of as a rare breed. She should have her papers and her health record. Never mind that now. You don't want her, I take it."

"You're dead right," he barked.

He was starting in again, but Leslie cut in.

"Did Tiffany try to train her?" she said crisply.

"We all tried. The animal is worthless, I tell you. I've promised to get Tiff a pedigreed, housebroken poodle. The kid is sick of cleaning up after Birdie-Brainless."

"How old is she exactly?" asked a voice Dickon had not heard before.

"About a year and a half. What does it matter?"

"Has she had her shots? Is she spayed?"

"Yeah, yeah. We had her fixed and generally checked out."

"How about a dog license?"

"No," he said uneasily.

"Get one for the poodle," Leslie Hawkin's voice said. "I'll take her now."

"Hey, I want that leash. I paid good money for it."

The children strained their ears, but heard nothing more for a few moments.

"I gotta go. I'm late," they heard him say finally.

"I also am late. If your daughter

cannot be kinder, do not get her that poodle."

"Wow," Anthony whispered. "She sounds fierce."

The children eyed each other and drifted back into the field. Dickon lingered until Jenny said, "Come on. She'd better not find you listening."

He trailed after her. Two minutes later, Leslie strode out to join them. Before they could ask her what was going to happen to Birdie, she spotted Dickon and frowned.

"I told you to go home," she snapped. Then her face softened. "You were a help with that poor dog and I'm grateful, but it's time you left."

Dickon gulped, turned on his heel and raced toward the fence. Then he braked and spun back to face her.

"What's going to happen to ... to Birdie?" he asked.

"We'll try to find her a home. But if she's as bad as the man says, it won't be easy. She's over a year old and not even housetrained. But she is appealing."

"Maybe ... maybe I could help her,"

Dickon said, knowing it made no sense.

"Will your family let you adopt her?"

"No," Dickon mumbled, staring at the ground. "My mother won't ... she got attacked ..."

"Then there's nothing you can do for her. Run along. We have work to do."

This time, Dickon went out the gate to the front, hoping to catch a last glimpse of Birdie. But the man was roaring away in his car and the Humane Society's front door was closed. There was no sign of the small dog with the flyaway ears.

"Birdie," he whispered. "I know how you feel."

Home again, he flung himself face down on the bed. He did not mean to cry, but once he started he couldn't stop.

Birdie needed him and he needed her. Yet there was not one thing he could do.

Apprentice Trainer

When he was quiet, at last, he heard the class working with their dogs next door.

"No, Tallboy. NO!" Daniel cried.

Dickon got up and slammed down the window. Without his glasses, everything outside blurred. He lay down on his bed again. Perhaps he should watch TV, he thought, but could not make himself go turn on the set.

Sleep rescued him.

At five o'clock, he woke, groggy and miserable. In the bathroom, he peered at himself in the mirror. His face was flushed and his eyelids were swollen. Mum must not see him looking like this. He ran the water as cold as he could get it and bathed his cheeks and eyes until he looked more himself. It was a good thing she was going to be late.

Then, all of a sudden, he wished she would come home right now.

"I need a hug," he told the mirror.

She was forever stretching out her arms and telling him that she needed a hug. He always gave her one even when he did not want to, but he had decided long ago that hugs should not be ordered up like pizza; they should just happen.

All the same, right now, he needed a bear hug from somebody. He remembered his dad's bear hugs and almost started crying again.

When his mother finally arrived, he was nearly asleep again in the big chair in front of the TV. She thought that he was slow and dragging because he was only half awake. He was glad. He could never tell her about Birdie. She would probably state right out that she had always said dogs were a lot of trouble. She would not understand how much he loved this one dog.

The next afternoon, Dickon tried not to look out the window. He didn't think he could bear to watch. But he could not keep his mind on anything else. They thought that all he had to do was take his pill and he would be able to focus, but it wasn't true. Sometimes nothing helped. His thoughts scattered in all directions like marbles spilled on the floor.

He was lying face down on his bed, punching his pillow, when the doorbell rang.

"Who is it?" he called through the door. He felt silly hesitating, but Mum had made him promise never to open it until he checked.

"Me. Jody. Open up, Dickon Bird."

Startled, Dickon swung the door back.

Jody, with Poppet beside her, stood grinning at him.

He pushed his glasses up to see her better and said not a word.

"Hey, Dickon," she said. "You know that dog Birdie?"

It was not three o'clock yet. Why wasn't she at the class? He could not bear to discuss Birdie. He nodded instead.

Jody chuckled. "You look as though you think I'm going to go off like a firecracker."

Poppet was wagging her tail hard. Dickon bent to scratch behind her ears. His hair flopped forward, hiding his face from Jody's teasing glance.

"What about Birdie?" he got out.

"How would you like to join our class and give that poor dog some training?" Jody asked, her eyes sparkling. "I suggested it and we all talked Leslie around. What do you say?"

"You're kidding!" Dickon burst out, unable to bear it. His hands shook and his heart pounded, as though his ribs caged a full set of drums. "It's mean to make fun about Birdie."

"Hey, what do you think I am?" She sounded really hurt.

"How should I know? I only met you once," Dickon said.

"Let me in and I'll explain," Jody said. "Let's not blow it before we start."

Mrs. Nelson was peering at them from next door. Dickon waved. She waved back and left the window.

"Come on in, then," he told the wild girl. He felt as though he would burst into tears any minute. But Jody wasn't like the Bridgeman brothers. Poppet loved her.

She followed him to the kitchen. He watched in amazement as she picked a tumbler out of the draining board, filled it with cold water and chugged it down. Then she straddled a chair and took a deep breath.

"Now listen. That little dog was abused by the girl who owned her. She is so nervous that finding her a new home will be hard. She shivers when she is touched and pees when she's scared, which is when anybody comes too close.

We got talking to Leslie about her and she told us how afraid she is that she won't be able to place her. Leslie thinks she should not be with a girl, not after that Tiffany. So Jenny and Kristin and I reminded her how different she was with you. She ran straight to you, remember? So, finally, Leslie said you could come over and we could try her in the class with the others. Maybe, just maybe, with our dogs near and you petting her, she'll calm down."

Jody's eyes were fixed on his face.

"Are you serious?" he whispered.

"Come on, Dickon, would I come if I weren't? What kind of kids did you hang around with where you came from?"

Dickon did not answer. She was waiting impatiently. She had no idea that the offer was like one of those dreams you stumble into without knowing your part.

"Well, yes or no?"

"Are you sure it's not a ... trick?"

"Positive. Leslie says you can come into our class and work with her for a week or two and see if she shapes up.

If she doesn't, nobody will adopt her and it'll be 'Bye-bye, Birdie.'"

"But I don't know how," Dickon said miserably.

"Me neither!" Jody grinned. "That's why we're in the class. Come on, Dickon Chicken, go for it."

Dickon stared at her. Nobody had ever called him Dickon Chicken – and he should be furious. But he did not mind one bit.

Suddenly he raced away from the kitchen, circled the small living room, dashed through the hallway and fetched up facing Jody again.

"Woweee!" he yelled.

Jody's mouth dropped open.

"Holy Nellie," she said, laughing. "Is that 'Yes'?"

"Yes," he shrieked. "Yes, yes, yes, YES!"

"Cool it, kid. It's not a trip to Canada's Wonderland. It's work. Leslie thinks you're too young. But I told her you were just small for your age. Stand still. You're making me dizzy."

"Yeah, okay, of course, whatever you

say," Dickon rattled off. He did his best to calm down. "When should I come?"

"Right now. They've been waiting for ages."

Dickon, dazed but joyful, was about to follow her when he realized he had not taken his medication at two o'clock. He raced into the bathroom and gulped the pill down.

Everyone was in the circle. Leslie had Birdie on a leash. The dog had been brushed, but she still looked scruffy. Her head drooped. So did her tail. Only her ears stayed tall. She did not notice Dickon coming across the grass.

Leslie gave him the leash and waited to see what would happen. "Here's your personal trainer, Birdie," she said.

"Hi, Birdie," Dickon said huskily.

The little dog started violently at the sound of Dickon's voice. "It's only me," the boy said, holding himself still.

She glanced up timidly. Then she came to life. Next thing they knew, she was bouncing on her hind feet with her front paws waving frantically, leaping for his knees. Her tall ears quivered. Her tail curled up and spun in circles. She saw him as her friend.

Dickon knelt and stroked her, murmuring love words.

"What did your mother say?" Leslie's voice asked above him.

"Nothing," said Dickon truthfully, his eyes on Birdie. "It's okay."

Jody's eyes gleamed, but she said nothing.

"All right. Once she's calm enough, do exactly what I tell you. You'll have to stay focussed. You look awfully young. You remind me of ... Well, never mind."

"I'll be twenty-one any minute," Dickon joked. Wild joy bubbled up inside him. He had seen a movie about geysers like Old Faithful shooting up out of the ground. He knew how the ground felt.

Giving Birdie a last pat, he rose and backed slowly toward the circle, drawing the tiny dog after him. When they got to their spot in the ring, he went down again on one knee, and petted her amazing ears. She seemed to relax a bit, but she still quivered slightly from nose to tail.

"Easy, girl," he told her softly, as he had the day before. "Nobody will hurt you. I won't let them. You are safe with me."

He straightened up and looked at Leslie. She studied him with cool eyes. Then she smiled.

"Maybe those girls are smarter than they look," she said. "Welcome to the class, Dickon Bird, apprentice trainer."

He squared his skinny shoulders and nodded. He would not let it go wrong.

Birdie in Training

"You have the right touch with her," Leslie continued. "After what she's been through, winning her trust might have taken much longer. Now, everybody, keep still and listen closely."

Dickon tried to contain the enormous sigh of relief and jubilation that pushed up out of him. Standing still was hard. Listening was even harder.

Leslie's words flew at him like swarms of butterflies. Birdie needed him to stay with it.

How was he going to manage? Then he saw Jody grinning at him and he knew. If he copied her every move, he'd do it right. If she got in trouble with Poppet, he'd look to Jenny and Perkins. Perkins was better behaved than Poppet. He gazed at Jenny as though she were Wonder Woman.

Dickon smiled at Birdie again and murmured, "Good girl."

Leslie had just told them they must heap on the praise.

"There is no such thing as too much praise," she said.

He liked that. He stopped listening as he smiled at his marvelous dog. Birdie was going to be ...

"Dickon, are you with us or not?"

His face burned.

"I am," he said. "I'm listening. I just am not used to being here yet."

Jody and Kristin laughed. Trevor and Jake did too. Last of all, Leslie herself grinned.

"I can see that might be a problem," she said. "I'm not quite used to it either! Now pull Birdie in to your left side and tell her to sit. As you say the word, press your left hand gently down on her rump and hold her head up with your right. Don't jerk it. We just want her to keep the commands 'Sit' and 'Down' separate. Wait. I'm not through. The minute she does sit, praise her as though she just won a gold medal."

Dickon pulled Birdie close. Much to his relief, she came and even leaned her slight weight against his leg.

"Sit," he said firmly. "Birdie, sit."

He reached down to encourage her, but she was already sitting. Her big eyes gazed anxiously up at him.

"Praise her NOW, Dickon," Leslie said.

Oh, yes. Praise her.

"Good girl, Birdie. Good, good girl!" he crooned.

She sprang up. Her tail quivered. As he beamed down at her, the tip of her tail spun in a little circle. Birdie was happy to be with him. For the moment, at least, she was his.

"Now, try it again, Dickon, and when she is sitting, tell her to stay. Keep your hand ready to encourage her. That goes for everybody. Birdie isn't the only one who sat for just three seconds."

Dickon was tired when it was over. And he was the only one who had to leave his dog behind.

"Can I take her in to her place?" he asked.

"Sure," Leslie said. "Good idea."

When he lifted her, he was amazed at how light she was.

"Yes," Leslie said. "She's much too thin. But we'll soon fix that."

He put her in the cage and closed the door. She gave him a reproachful look. Leslie laughed.

"Dogs are experts at making people feel guilty," she said. "I was watching her. She must have had some training before that man got her. She would have been young, of course, but Papillons are highly intelligent. I've seen them win at Obedience Trials."

Birdie whined softly when he turned to go.

"I'll be back tomorrow. Bye-bye, Birdie," he told her.

The next morning was Friday. It seemed years since the Friday before. He hadn't known Leslie or Jody or Birdie then!

At ten, he went back over, rounding the building. The small woman he had seen outside with Leslie on his first day in the new house was at the desk working on some papers. He opened the door and looked at her bent head. He was relieved to see Leslie coming out of the room where all the dogs were. She spotted him and smiled.

"Hi, Dickon," she said. "This is Sally Croft. Can one of us do something for you?"

Dickon swallowed. Then he looked up into her cool eyes.

"Birdie's still pretty tangled," he said, all in a rush. "If she is going to get adopted, maybe I should brush her."

Leslie studied him silently for what

felt like at least half an hour. Then she said quietly, "It would be great for Birdie, Dickon, but maybe not so good for you. If you bond with her, she'll be hard to give up."

"I won't bond," Dickon said, ready to promise anything.

"Well, all right then. That little dog sure needs to become more trusting. She shouldn't be too hard to groom. Papillons have no undercoat and they don't mat like most breeds. Their hair is like ours."

She went with him to the cage where Birdie lay with her head on her paws. She looked so lost that a lump formed in Dickon's throat.

"Hi, Birdie," he half-sang in his softest voice.

The woman let the little dog out. "My, she's thin," she said. "Sally gave her a flea bath this morning, but she hasn't had time to groom her. Here's your friend Dickon, Birdie."

The dog trembled violently in Leslie's arms. She shook in Dickon's arms too. But he held her gently and kept saying her name in a soft sing-song. She ducked her head to lick his fingers, but he could tell she was still anxious, not sure his kindness would last.

"Healing takes time," Leslie said, watching them. "She's bruised, Dickon, in both her heart and her body. Go slowly with her. Be patient."

"Yes," Dickon answered, only half attending. He sat down on the floor with Birdie cradled close. He kept murmuring what a good dog she was, how special, how beautiful.

Leslie brought grooming tools. She led the boy and dog into a room with a grooming table and two deep sinks for bathing. Birdie had begun to relax, but she did not want another bath.

"It's all right," Leslie told her, laughing as the little dog put her paws around Dickon's neck and hid her eyes under his chin. "Let me show you what to do, Dickon."

She placed Birdie on the table, but the dog became so agitated Dickon took her back into his arms.

"I can keep her on my lap and do

it since she's so little," he said.

"All right." The woman showed him how to brush out the tangles without hurting the small dog. Then she left the pair to get on with it.

Dickon thought it might be a battle, but Birdie leaned her head against the stroking brush. He pulled it slowly and carefully through her damp tangles. He found a sore spot on her right flank. Her ribs were tender too, and she would not let him handle one of her slim paws. She even growled at him, but only in warning.

"Poor little Bird," he murmured. "I won't hurt you. How could they do this? Did someone kick you?"

Leslie came back to check on them just as he finished.

"You are doing a wonderful job, Dickon, but you must always remember that she is not yours or you'll break both your hearts when she's adopted."

Dickon bent his head low over the dog. So that was what bonding meant. It was too late. It had been too late since he and Birdie had first laid eyes upon one another. His heart belonged to this dog. And he was positive that Birdie's heart was his. They were stuck to each other tighter than Crazy Glue could make them and that was that.

Mrs. Nelson and Mrs. Fielding

The weekend dragged. Luckily, his mother was still busy setting the house to rights. The two of them painted his bedroom pale yellow. It took several coats, but Dickon got to do a lot of the work.

Then Monday came and he was back with Birdie. When he raced home, however, happy as he could be, Mrs. Nelson was sitting on his front step.

His feet skidded to a stop.

"Stop right there, young man," she said. " I've been watching you for a week. I know what you are up to and I also know your mother has no notion."

"Oh, please, PLEASE, don't tell her!" Dickon begged. He dropped to his knees in front of their neighbor and gazed up at her. "Mum wouldn't understand. She's afraid of dogs. I can't have one. But Birdie needs me. She really does. Leslie ..."

Mrs. Nelson reached out a hand and gave him a quick shake.

"Never grovel!" she said. "Leslie is my husband's niece. I called her after the second day. She says you are doing a good job with that poor little dog."

Dickon scrambled to his feet. A smile beamed across his face.

"She does? Really? She really does?"

"She really does. She thinks the dog may be able to be adopted if your mother doesn't stop your going over there."

"Oh, Mrs. Nelson ..." he started in.

"Hush. I haven't told Julie yet. I know she has a phobia about dogs.

She doesn't want to risk one hair of your foolish head. One of these days, we will have to tell. But Leslie thinks another few days may settle this Birdie down enough."

Dickon felt a warmth in his heart and a pain in his stomach. Birdie might be all right! But he would lose her. How could he bear it?

"Julie will be home soon. I'm surprised she hasn't smelled dogs on you. She must come home very tired indeed."

"She does," Dickon said, giving their neighbor a sheepish grin. "I watch for the car and push the button on the coffeemaker. She takes in this great deep breath and smells fresh coffee. I change my shirt too, and I wash when I get home."

Mrs. Nelson laughed.

"Very tricky," she said. "Come and see Charlie when you want a change of animals."

"Thanks," Dickon said. "How come she has a boy's name?"

"It's short for Charlotte. That's Leslie's second name. She gave her to me a couple of years ago. Someone had brought her in to the Humane Society and Leslie wanted her to go to an adult. African pygmy hedgehogs are not ideal pets for a child."

Dickon decided it was too late to visit Charlie right then. He had to put the coffee in the filter and pour in the water.

Mrs. Nelson headed home.

Leslie had told her aunt that Birdie was making great progress. His pleasure faded. If he did a super job with Birdie, he would lose her sooner.

The rest of the second week passed, though, and they began on the third without anyone wanting Birdie.

And Dickon's mother had not caught on. She was tired, of course. The manager, Mr. Frank, was picky sometimes. When she got home, his mother had to tell Dickon the latest adventure they had had. She said she had to be careful because she could not afford to get fired. Dickon knew there was no danger of that happening. His mother was smart and she worked hard.

"How was Mr. Frankenstein today?" he would ask her.

She would shake her head at him, but she always smiled.

One night when she asked about his day, Dickon told her about going over to see Charlie having her bath.

"Oh, honey, do be careful," she warned. "That hedgehog might seem as friendly as can be and then take a piece out of you."

"Charlie is a pushover," he said impatiently. "Anyway, her prickles make me keep my distance so don't fuss."

"I can't help it," she said, pushing buttons on the microwave. "I know she's not a dog, but when I was three ..."

"You've told me a million times," he broke in, unable to hide his sudden anger. "But dogs are okay. They are fine. Otherwise, Mum, why would hundreds of people buy them for their kids? Answer me that."

She stared into his face. He was not sounding like himself. His cheeks reddened and he looked away.

"Maybe we should get a small

aquarium and some of those Japanese koi," she said, staring at him. "I know it is nice to have a pet. Koi are all different colors. You might enjoy ..."

He could not believe it.

"No, Mother," he said. "I do not desire a wet pet. Or a gerbil or a mouse or a guinea pig. For me, it's a dog or nothing."

Silence came between them. He gritted his teeth and made no move to break through it. His mother sighed.

"Do you feel all right, baby?" she asked at last. "You must get so bored shut up with only the TV. We'll forget fish for now. I brought you a present, something to help pass the time. It's so cute."

He opened the paper bag and pulled out a sticker book. He stared down at it. It was about toys. Teddy bears. The one on the cover was like the one on his stupid baby cup. He pushed the book away and tried to change the subject back to hedgehogs.

"Mrs. Nelson lets Charlie ride around in her apron pocket," he said.

His mother shuddered. All at once, he wanted to hit her. He longed to burst out, "Birdie is a wonderful dog and I am training her and Leslie says she is doing wonderfully well and I've taught her to stay and sit and she almost always comes when I say, 'Birdie, come!' She knows more than Ruff and she is far better than Tallboy although Poppet is better at some things. But Jody had already worked with her before the class began. Oh, Mum, Mum, MUM, I never ever did anything so wonderful before. Never, ever, EVER!"

He bit back the flood of words. If he told, she might forbid him to go near the Humane Society. She was staring at him now with bewildered eyes.

"Did you take your pill at two?" she asked.

He felt like a time bomb ticking down to the moment when it would blow sky-high.

"YES! I am fine as fine as fine," he shouted, leaping up and rushing to pour himself a glass of water. The chair fell over with a crash, and when he turned the tap on, water sprayed in all directions.

"Oh, baby, watch what you're doing!" she wailed. But he saw relief in her face. She knew this boy. He was hers.

Maybe she wanted him to stay this way. Did she like his being her own special wild Birdie? If she saw him with the others, acting like everybody else, would she want to change him back to Dizzy Dick? He could not bear the thought.

"I'm watching every minute. It's only water, Mum. It's not the end of the blasted world. It's not dire. And I'm OKAY. Don't make a big production out of it," he said, struggling to stay in control.

"I'm sorry, baby," she said, her eyes filling with the tears he so hated. "I know you're trying hard. But you'll have to get yourself to settle down if you are to go to the regular school, Birdie."

Don't call me "Birdie," he thought. Don't call me "baby" either.

"I KNOW!" he cried aloud, his eyes wild. "Don't you think I know anything?

I'm weird. Your weird kid. So weird I can't even have a dog like other kids."

His last few words had dropped to a whisper. Had she heard? No. She had turned to get out two frozen dinners. If she had caught what he had whispered, she would just say for the millionth time that he could not possibly take care of a dog — even if he could find one who was guaranteed not to be vicious or dirty. If Birdie were frightened, how could he be sure what she would do?

"I gotta pee," he cried, and ran, shutting the bathroom door behind him. For the first time in his life, he locked it. He needed to have a minute really truly to himself.

No, that wasn't it. He needed time to BE his new self. Not "Julie's baby bird" but Dickon Fielding.

"Are you all right?" she called.

He flushed the toilet, splashed water on his hands and face and unlocked the door.

"Of course," he told her.

They Might Want Birdie

The next morning, his mother felt his forehead.

"Open your mouth wide," she told him. "I think you must be coming down with something."

"I feel great," he said, frantic to get her gone. " Maybe I stayed out too long in the sun yesterday."

"Bird, where were you? You promised to stay inside the house while I'm at work. How could you get too much sun?"

His thoughts skidded into each other like bumper cars at the midway. But, just in time, he pounced on one that saved him.

"Mrs. Nelson took me over to watch Charlie have a bath," he said. "I was out with her while she was drying off in the sunshine. She's so cute, the way she stretches out."

"All right. I just can't help worrying about you. Well, if you really are fine, I must fly or I'll be there late. Does she really bathe a hedgehog?"

He nodded, smiled and opened the front door for her. After she drove away, he counted to one hundred three times. Then he took off.

Here I come, Birdie, his heart sang. Here I come, girl.

He went straight to where the brushes were kept and got what he needed to groom his dog. But when he went to the cage, it was empty.

He felt as though a giant hand was

squeezing the life out of him. For several seconds, he stood frozen, staring at the cage. Then he ran to the desk. Leslie was there. She beamed at him although her eyes were not smiling.

"Where's Birdie?" he croaked.

"A couple is looking for a pet," she said. "They're walking with two dogs. They have Birdie now and then they'll take Pickles."

She saw the horror in his eyes.

"I was afraid of this, Dickon. Birdie can't spend her life in a cage, even with you visiting her each day. She deserves a home and family. If your mother would take her, that would be perfect, but you say she won't."

At that moment, the people came back with Birdie. She was overjoyed to see Dickon. He knelt down and picked her up, hiding his face in her silky coat.

"This is the boy I was telling you about. He's done a great job with Birdie. But let's put a leash on Pickles. He's a little more ... Well, a happier dog. He's younger too. About ten months old, the vet thinks."

"Yes," the lady said, smiling a sugary smile. "Birdie is darling, of course, but she's a bit skittish."

"She's too small to be a real dog," the man muttered.

Pickles wagged her tail so hard it was comical. She was twice Birdie's size.

"We really wanted a larger dog. Pickles is just right," the lady said, taking the leash.

Dickon held Birdie close and turned his back on the couple so they would not be tempted. Why would anyone choose that brainless Pickles over Birdie?

He and Leslie glanced at each other. They watched the couple going down the sidewalk with Pickles bouncing along next to them. She pulled ahead and stopped to sniff bushes.

"I should have given you Pickles to work on in the Obedience Class," Leslie said. "She's young yet, but she's going to be a handful."

"I don't like her," Dickon said, cuddling Birdie close.

"Sure you do. Nobody could dislike

Pickles. Anyway, you're not going to lose that little dog today. But prepare yourself! Birdie is lovable and attractive. She's almost ready to be adopted, Dickon. Someone is sure to want her."

"I'd take her myself," Sally said. "But my husband says four dogs are enough."

"Especially when two of them are beagles," Leslie said.

"What's wrong with beagles?" Dickon asked unsteadily.

"Well, Sally's two have dreams of running away and making their fortunes," Leslie said.

Dickon's thoughts were not on Sally's beagles. "Someone is sure to want her," Leslie had said. Well, someone already does, he thought fiercely.

"Pickles is the one for us," the lady said, beaming. "She's darling."

"Reminds me of a dog I had as a boy," her husband said.

Neither glanced at Birdie peering over Dickon's shoulder. She stretched out her paw as though to shake hands, but they did not notice. Dickon pulled the paw down fast.

They left.

Dickon began grooming Birdie with special care. Nobody else would come. Surely he could at least finish up the Dog Training classes before anyone would take her. Birdie was doing so well, but she was not perfect yet.

"Leslie, can't you just not let people look at Birdie until the classes are done?" he asked, keeping his head bent.

"There's only a week left," she said. "I'll try. But the week will pass, Dickon. And it will be just as hard then."

He said nothing. She sighed.

"Tomorrow's the day we test the dogs in obedience class," Leslie reminded him a week later. "I hope Birdie does you proud."

Dickon hoped so too. Tomorrow. He had not realized that the class was almost over. Well, maybe he had, but he had forced his thoughts to keep away from the subject. He went home and tried to eat the lunch his mother had left for him, but he could not finish. That afternoon, everyone worked hard.

"I don't want the training to end," Jenny said. "Perkins is doing fine, but couldn't we go on and work toward those Obedience Trials they have at dog shows? I went once with my aunt and it was cool."

Leslie looked thoughtful.

"Maybe we could consider offering an advanced class," she said slowly.

Dickon's heart leapt and then he remembered. Birdie was not his. If they had this advanced class, he would have no dog to train.

He wakened on Friday knowing the day of testing had come. What if Birdie blew it?

"You have to eat more than that," Mum said, looking at his plate. "Are you sick? Should I stay home?"

"No." he yelped, in panic. "I was just resting."

He stuffed in some toast.

Then she was gone and he ran to pick up Birdie. A friend of Leslie was the judge. She looked serious. Dickon crossed his fingers and wished.

Birdie was practically perfect. She sat when he told her to sit. She stayed and then she came to him, circling behind him and sitting down on his left side. She walked at heel as though she had never done anything else.

Dickon felt smug. Tallboy had done almost everything sloppily and had refused to come until he had had two leash corrections. Poppet kept lying down when she was supposed to be sitting. Little Hercules tripped Kristin up. Dog after dog did something wrong. But not his Birdie.

Only "Sit ... stay" was left, the command where he would walk away from her, wait one minute and call her to him. She loved doing this one. It was her best thing.

"Sit, Birdie. Stay!" he said firmly, giving her the hand signal.

Head high, he strode away.

Jingle, jingle. Somebody's rabies tag and dog license were clinking together.

Not Birdie's, he told himself, staring straight ahead.

The other kids were laughing. A dog was dancing at his heels. He turned his head ever so slightly to check.

She was right behind him, looking proud of herself.

"Oh, Birdie, no!" he wailed.

"Try again," Leslie said, "even though she has already lost the points."

"We've all had this experience," the judge said kindly. "Perhaps she's a bit young."

She wasn't. Blushing, he reseated his dog and told her again what to do. This time she remained exactly where he had left her.

"Birdie, COME!" he called.

When she romped over to him, he was still so proud of her he wanted to hug her.

Leslie handed him a certificate. She also gave him a dog biscuit. "You two have surely earned this," she said.

The other kids clapped. Dickon had never been so proud.

"Time to eat," Sally said, smiling at them.

Then Dickon glanced through the

wire fence into his own backyard. Mrs.
Nelson was watching.

Next to her stood his mother.

Battle is Joined

Dickon thrust the leash at Leslie.

"I gotta go," he gasped.

"But, Dickon ... " she began.

"My mother's there," he whispered and ran. He dashed around the Humane Society building and raced home.

"Mum, Mum," he shouted, "I can explain. Birdie needed me. Leslie will tell you ..."

He broke off. She wasn't there.

"Where are you?" he shrieked.

She came out of the bathroom. Her head was bent. She had been crying. He saw her grip her hands together to stop them shaking.

"I trusted you," she said in a small tight voice.

"I know, Mum, but you don't understand. Wait till I tell you."

"Don't bother. Amy Nelson has already told me. She knew. I trusted her too. You both betrayed ..."

Her words choked on a hiccupy sob. She turned her back on him. Her shoulders heaved.

He knew, with a sick feeling, that she meant him to see her like that, just as she wanted him to hear that ugly word "betray."

Dickon was beside himself. If only she would listen! He was in big trouble. Maybe he deserved to be. He had disobeyed her.

But he had not lied. Not in words anyway.

"I've put macaroni and cheese in

to heat. Leave me alone until it's ready," she said.

Her bedroom door shut in his face. He stood there numb with shock. What should he do? He gritted his teeth. Well, he would not cry. She hadn't listened. His anger was a tight knot in his chest. His throat ached.

The phone rang. Was she going to get it? No. He picked the receiver up on the sixth ring.

"Hello," he said. His voice sounded far away.

"Julie?"

"No," he said, recognizing Mrs. Nelson's voice. "It's me, Dickon. She's lying down. She said to leave her alone."

"Well, I don't know what all the fuss is about. Surely a boy has a right to go next door and help train a needy dog. You weren't out of sight of my window once. Tell her to call me when she gets up."

He hung up, feeling braver. Somebody was on his side.

All at once, he knew that he was not the one who should be saying "sorry."

His mother had been unfair. She had made up her mind that he was bad without giving him a chance to speak. He stomped back out the front door, slamming it behind him, and kicked the step until his toes hurt.

In that instant, he decided. He was not baby Birdie, Julie's little Dickie Bird. Not any longer. He was Dickon Fielding. And about time too.

He shivered at his own daring, but he had made up his mind. He was going to fight her for Birdie. And he was going to win.

The door opened.

"Oh," his mother said, startled. "I heard the door shut and I thought you'd run off ..."

Dickon faced her. He did not jiggle or jump. He did not plead either. He did not shed a tear. He spoke slowly, his voice rock steady.

"I want Birdie," he said.

"Birdie is that dog Amy Nelson was talking about, is it? Who decided on that name, if I may ask?" Her tone was icy.

"Not me," he yelled at her. "The kid who abused her thought her ears looked like wings. They do, too. She's a Papillon, Mum. It's the French word for butterfly. She's ..."

"This bird dog is no concern of ours," she broke in. "You know full well ..."

"She's going to be MY dog." He shot the words at her like bullets. "We are going to adopt her. If you don't let me, I will never forgive you."

Her mouth dropped open and the steel went out of her backbone.

"Birdie," she moaned, reaching out to him and letting tears rain down her face. "Please, stop speaking in that hard, cruel way. You look just like your father. You mustn't do this to me."

"I must," he told her. "For Birdie I can do even more. And why shouldn't I look like Dad? Most boys look like their dads."

"But, sweetheart, he left us ..."

"This isn't about Dad!" Dickon said desperately. "You have to meet Birdie. You have to come over there with me now, before somebody else takes her."

"You're forgetting how afraid I am."

He just looked at her and she faltered. Then she changed tack.

"You might be allergic ..."

He dashed past her into the kitchen and snatched up the teddy bear cup. She followed.

"You know I'm not. And you know I'm too old for teddy bear cups too." He dropped it into the garbage bin.

"Oh, don't," she sniffled.

"Blow your nose, Mum," said her son. He stood still, studying her, and then he astonished her and himself by leaning forward and kissing her wet cheek. He must have grown a lot since school let out. He hardly had to stretch up at all.

"Come on. Come with me to meet Birdie."

He turned his back and marched out the door. After a moment, to his amazed delight, he heard his mother stumbling after him.

Homecoming

The kids and Sally Croft had gone, but the door swung open under Dickon's eager hand.

"Birdie, wait ..." his mother called, her voice breathless. He pretended not to hear. Leslie glanced up from cleaning up cookie crumbs and spills of juice. Her eyes widened at Dickon and then widened even more as his mother came in.

"Dickon, did you forget something?" she said.

"This is my mother," he burst out, ignoring the question. "My real name is Dickon Fielding. Jody got it wrong by mistake and I never told her. Mum's name is Julie Fielding. We've come to see Birdie."

"You mean ..."

"I want Mum to meet her. She has to understand why we have to take her home."

He thought it best to hide his doubts. Leslie hesitated, staring at his mother as though she did not believe such a woebegone-looking woman would be a good person to adopt a dog. She hesitated.

"Please, Leslie," Dickon begged. "Let me show her."

"All right, Dickon," she said then. "This way, Mrs. Fielding."

She led them back to the room where the dogs were kept. Julie Fielding got as far as the door and froze. But her son did not see her. He unlatched Birdie's cage and the little dog came to him, putting her tiny paws up around his neck. He scooped her into his arms and held her close.

"Isn't she beautiful, Mum?" he said, stroking the small dog lovingly. "Isn't she perfect?"

Julie Fielding was amazed at how small and dainty Dickon's dog was. Her ears seemed to be sending signals to her boy's mother. Little flips of greeting that almost made Julie smile in spite of herself.

"I thought she was a stray," she said. "She looks like a rare breed."

"She is," Leslie Hawkin said. "Papillons are getting better known, though. They go way back in history. Marie Antoinette had one."

Something in Julie Fielding's expression made hope stir in Dickon's heart. The decision wasn't made yet, though. Leslie had questions to ask. So did Dickon's mother.

"Is the dog housebroken?"

"Yes," Leslie said firmly. "Birdie is beautifully behaved or she will be when she settles. Often dogs make mistakes just at first in a new home because they don't know what is expected of them. They get tense. When she first arrived, she leaked when anyone looked at her, but she's so much happier now. Dickon has convinced her that the world is a friendly place."

She smiled at Dickon. He tried to smile back, but his lips felt wooden. He was too nervous to pretend to be calm. His eyes darted from one face to the other and back again. Who was this Marie?

"Birdie was badly abused by her previous owners," Leslie added. "At first, she was frightened of everyone. But your son has worked wonders with her. You should be proud of him."

Even though she was saying good things, Dickon wished she wouldn't keep on and on. He almost interrupted to tell them to hurry up. Then he saw how much calmer his mother was growing as she listened to the story of how he and Birdie had come together. He clamped his lips shut. As the minutes crawled past, the set look left her face.

He wanted to hug her. The next instant, he wanted to clap his hand over her mouth.

"My Dickon is a special needs child," she blurted out. He braced himself.

His mother went on, "He takes medication daily and that helps, but he has trouble concentrating ..."

"ADHD? My brother Jeremy has the same trouble," Leslie said matter-of-factly, startling them both. "Dickon put me in mind of Jeremy from the start. He's going to a community college now, with special help, of course. Your son did seem pretty wild and woolly at first, but working with Birdie made a huge difference in him. He had to stay focussed, you see, and he knew he must not frighten her. After all, she's a special needs dog."

Dickon longed to race around the room in dizzy circles, but with an enormous effort he stayed still and tried to look modest. Leslie chuckled. Even his mother smiled.

Silence fell, a silence filled with waiting. Dickon thought he would burst before his mother spoke at last.

"Well, maybe we could take her over the weekend as a trial," Julie Fielding said faintly. She sounded scared and Dickon knew he should comfort her. Instead he leaped into the air and gave a whoop of delight. The little dog clutched to his chest began to tremble violently. He pulled himself together fast before Mum changed her mind.

When they left the Humane Society, he led Birdie on a leash and Julie Fielding carried her papers and enough food to keep her supplied for a couple of days. Neither spoke during the short walk. They reached the small, crowded house.

Mrs. Nelson was just turning away from their front door.

"My heavens!" she gasped. "What have you two been up to while my back was turned?"

"We are the Fielding family, now complete with dog," Dickon's mother said, a little stiffly. "She is called Birdie, as I suspect you know."

"Two birdies in one house," Amy Nelson said, grinning.

Then, she hugged her neighbor, dog food and all.

"You're a brick after all, Julie Fielding," she said.

"I'm a lunatic," said Dickon's mother weakly. "We're only trying this out over the weekend. No decisions have been made. Oh, the macaroni must be dried out."

"I went in with my key and rescued it," Amy Nelson said, blushing faintly.

"You were going to march in and give me a piece of your mind," Julie Fielding said. "But my son saved you the trouble."

She hadn't called him Birdie. He opened his mouth to say something and then shut it. He had his dog. He could afford to give her time.

A Real Dog

Dickon was so happy that once he had Birdie safely inside his own house he shot around the small rooms like a Catherine wheel. He yelped out cheers and fell to his knees to hug his new dog.

"Birdie," his mother gasped. "What if you scare her? She may go for you. Do take care."

Dickon laughed and twirled around

on his bottom for good measure.

"You won't go for me, Birdie, will you?" he sang out, grinning down at his new pet, his first pet, his one and only dog. "Her jaws are too delicate to take a chunk out of anybody. Besides, she's a lady."

He was right. She did not go for him. In her fear, she squatted and let go a puddle of pee on the kitchen floor. Then her tail went between her legs and she whimpered, waiting to be punished. In one shamed second she seemed to forget all the weeks of loving and brushing and training. All she remembered was the man who had struck her and shouted at her.

"Oh, Birdie! Poor Birdie," Dickon cried, stricken. "I'm sorry, girl. You didn't mean to do it. Mum, look at her trembling."

His mother could not help but see. She saw the puddle, the frightened small dog and her son who was no longer all hers. Well, now he must see that she had been quite right about dogs dirtying up the place. He MUST see.

If Dickon saw Birdie's disgraceful

puddle, he clearly was not planning to clean it up at once. He sat next to his dog and pulled her onto his lap, crooning comforting things.

His nervous mother watched him with a look as loving as his for Birdie. Never before had she seen him so tender with anyone except herself. Never before had she seen him so grown-up. So normal.

She felt confused, her emotions flip-flopping back and forth between delight and resentment. What was happening to her baby bird?

Whatever it was, the puddle still waited. She sighed a little more loudly than she needed to and started to go for a cloth.

"I'll do it," Dickon said, leaping up so fast that Birdie tumbled off his knees onto the hard floor. The little dog gave a startled yip, but the boy's attention stayed on the task. He grabbed the cloth and mopped up the floor. Then he stared at the cloth. His nose wrinkled up.

"What'll I do with it? Where should I throw it out?"

His mother looked at his disgusted expression and laughed.

"Rinse it out in the toilet and hang it out on the line for next time," she said. "We don't have dozens of floor cloths."

"In the ... toilet?"

"That's right. Where do you think mothers rinse out diapers?"

"They don't," Dickon said firmly. "They use disposables. I've seen them on TV."

"Well, if you think this dog you prize so highly will wear a disposable diaper ..." she said, grinning in spite of herself.

"Okay, okay." He cut her off and vanished into the bathroom.

Birdie whimpered and then, bravely, stood up and went after him, making a big detour to get past Julie.

Boy and dog returned.

"Did you see that? She followed me," Dickon boasted.

"I saw. You go fix up a bed for her. She'd better sleep in the kitchen."

"She can sleep in my room."

"No, she cannot. It isn't healthy. She'll be fine in the kitchen. And if you want her to stay, shouldn't you take off her leash?"

"Sorry, girl," Dickon murmured and undid the clip.

Julie Fielding held her breath, ready for Birdie to fly away or leap at his throat. But the little dog stayed close to Dickon, sniffing at his laces.

He found an old clothes basket, put a thick towel into it and patted it down.

"Jump in, Birdie," he said. "Come on, my sweet Birdie."

She sniffed the outside of the basket and then leaped in, turned around twice and lay down.

"Brilliant Birdie. See how she likes it," he began.

Before the words were out of his mouth, his dog had tipped the basket over, scrambling out, and set off to explore the rest of the small kitchen.

Julie soon realized that the kitchen was not going to work. Birdie made her too nervous underfoot like that. And the basket took up too much space.

The bathroom was even smaller.

"You win," she told her son. "Move her bed into your room. But remember, you sleep in your bed and she sleeps in hers."

"Of course," Dickon said, his eyes gleaming.

He looked for his pup. Where was she? How did you keep track of a dog who only knew how to heel and stay and come when she was on her leash? How could he make her behave without Leslie's help?

He found her in his room, chewing up a piece of Lego. When he rushed to rescue it, she backed away and squatted.

"Oh, no!" he moaned.

During supper, she chewed up one of the sealskin moccasins his father had brought him after a trip to the Arctic. Dickon took what was left away from her and hid it deep in his wastebasket. He scolded her in an angry whisper. The confused little dog began to squat once more.

Dickon's mother shrieked and Dickon

grabbed the sinner and shot outside with her. She dribbled all the way.

"Oh, Birdie, NO," her boy moaned.

Ten minutes later, much to her new master's surprise, she started barking at the door.

"Nobody's there," he told her. The doorbell chimed.

Jody and Poppet stood outside.

"We heard the great news so we brought Birdie a homecoming present," Jody said. She handed Dickon a chew toy and two old tennis balls. Poppet looked at the balls as though she knew they were hers.

"Even though real dogs are much more bother than dream ones, real ones are way better once you get used to them," Jody said. "I thought about my first few days with Poppet and decided you might need me to promise you that it'll be fine."

"Thanks," Dickon said. "Did Poppet chew up things and pee on the floor?"

"Yup. She still chews up things every so often, but she never pees in the house now. I also brought you a book on dog raising. It's on loan."

"Thanks," Dickon said again.

He'd never be able to read such a fat book. Maybe Mum would read some of it to him.

"It has a couple of pages about Papillons in it," Jody said. "They go way back in history. Queens owned them. Well, you can read it yourself. There's a whole little book about Papillons at the pet store."

"Cool," Dickon said. Maybe that Marie was a queen.

"Call me at this number if you need help," she said, handing him a slip of paper. "I live just two streets over that way. Did you hear Jenny's idea about going on with Obedience Training? I think Leslie is going to do it if we are serious. My mother says it's okay with her. Even if the classes don't work out, we could start our own Dog Club. Would you like to join?"

He stared at her.

"Yeah," he said, his eyes shining. "I sure would."

"Good luck," Jody said and took off,

Poppet bouncing along next to her.

When he went back inside, he caught his mother looking at him as though she had never seen him before. She smiled.

"Is that girl your friend?" she asked softly.

Dickon hesitated. He understood why she was asking. None of the kids from school had ever dropped by like that. But he was not certain what to answer. Having a friend was so new. He was scared to talk about it in case it was not real. But finally he nodded.

"Yes," he said huskily. "I think some of the others kind of like me too."

His mother turned her eyes away from the wonder on his face and cleared her throat.

"That's nice," she said, keeping it light.

Dickon's "real" dog hopped in and out of her basket many times that night. Every time, she took care to wake him up. When he did go off to sleep at last, she sneaked up onto his bed. He woke to find her curled around his feet.

"Mum will have a fit," he whispered, but Birdie flew off the bed the moment she heard his mother stirring. She floated to the floor and landed like a feather. When Julie looked in, the tiny dog gazed up at her, innocent as an angel.

It was Saturday morning and Mum was staying home. Dickon went around feeling bubbly. He pestered his mother to admit Birdie was perfect, but she would not. Even so, he believed she was weakening. How could she not?

Then Birdie pooped behind the couch. She had whined at the door, but he had been watching a Batman video and not noticed.

"I can't take this!" his mother snapped. She gave Birdie a disgusted look and brandished the weekend paper at her.

"Bad dog!" she scolded.

Birdie stiffened and gave a small whir in her throat. It was too tiny to be called a growl, but it was the best she could do.

Julie Fielding backed away, her eyes wide.

"Did you hear that?" she demanded

shrilly. "We can't keep a dog who growls. If I hadn't pulled my hand back, she'd have bitten me."

"No," Dickon cried, putting his arm around his frightened dog. "She didn't mean it."

"Oh, didn't she? She's dirty and she is not to be trusted. You heard her snarl yourself. I warned you. No, don't try to clean up. You'll just make it worse."

She was pale and she did not look him in the eye.

"What are you saying?" he choked, his eyes enormous behind their glasses.

She had her back to him.

"I'm sorry, Bird. I really am. But nobody could expect me to put up with this. Messing in the house. Vicious behavior. She'll have to go back first thing Monday morning."

Birdie in Disgrace

Dickon stared at his mother. Surely he had heard her wrong!

"No, Mum. No," he whispered.

She turned, saw the shock on his face and rushed out of the room, leaving him and his fierce Papillon alone.

He took a deep breath and shut his mouth tight on a roar of anguish. She had left the mess untouched. He got up and got paper towels. The poop was loose and he knew why she had said he would make it messier. He would show her.

He picked up what he could. Then he got a cloth and washed the carpet over and over until it was cleaner than it had been before Birdie had dirtied it. He actually sniffed it to make sure he had done it right.

Birdie watched him, her head on one side, no curl in her tail. She looked as nervous as he felt. Even her ears seemed to have shrunk.

"It's all right, girl, but don't do it again," he told her.

She won't have a chance, a voice inside him said.

She will so, he replied.

But his mother was staying in her bedroom with the door shut for a long time.

Then the phone rang. He let it ring until she answered. Then he tiptoed close enough to listen.

"Don't ask," he heard her say. "I'm afraid she turned out to be vicious."

Silently, Dickon began to cry. Birdie was not vicious. He knew she wasn't. Mum had scared her; that was all. It was not fair.

He went on listening.

"I can't take the chance that she'll bite him." His mother's voice rose.

As if she would!

There was a pause. He heard a voice squawking through the phone line.

"Leslie, you say you know that this animal has not a vicious bone in her body. But she growled at me. Birdie will say so himself."

She dropped her voice then. No matter how hard Dickon strained to hear, he caught no more.

"Well, thanks for calling. I have to get my boy some supper now."

Her boy bolted across the room and sat with Birdie cradled in his arms.

Julie Fielding went straight to the kitchen, pretending not to see them. She came back with cleaning things and silently went to the spot behind the couch.

"I cleaned it up," he said hoarsely.

"I see you tried," she said, scrubbing busily at the clean carpet.

She couldn't even admit that he had done a good job.

He put on Birdie's leash and took her out. When she began to squat, he gently urged her over to the curb. Leslie had taught them to do this and Birdie remembered.

"Good, good girl!" Dickon heaped on the praise.

Supper was a silent meal. Mum had picked up a barbecued chicken, usually one of his favorite meals. Tonight it choked him. Once he tried bringing up the subject, but she refused to discuss it. After that, he was too wretched to talk. Besides, he was as mad as she was.

After they finished, she started taking the chicken off the bones. He pretended to watch TV while really rehearsing what to say the first chance he got. By the set of his mother's shoulders, he could tell that now was not the moment.

"Birdie, go to bed," she called.

He faced her, holding his dog in his

arms, and burst out, "Mum, I have to talk about Birdie. I have to."

She looked at his too-bright eyes, his flaming cheeks. She sighed.

"We'll discuss it in the morning," she said. "I need to sleep on it. Leslie thinks she's not vicious. But both you and I heard her growl."

"Mum, that was no growl! Listen to me!"

"Tomorrow," she said. "But don't hope too hard, son. I am afraid I have made up my mind. Not another word until morning."

Clutching Birdie, he ran to his room. For the first time she could remember, he did not kiss her goodnight.

And it was that dog's fault.

Saved

The house was very small. Julie Fielding, putting the meat away in the fridge, could hear her son sobbing.

"I can vouch for that dog's being gentle," Leslie Hawkin had said. "I remember the day she was brought in. The kids persuaded me to let Dickon help with her the very next day. He was too young but he reminded me of my brother Jeremy. Dickon was forlorn and they all liked him ... Well, never mind that. He came every day. He sometimes even arrived on weekends when there were no classes, although he was in a hurry then."

"He must have gone while I was out shopping," Julie had said slowly.

"The point is," Leslie said, not letting her finish, "that little dog never once even snapped at anybody. She was nervous. Nervous dogs often do snap. But once Dickon worked with her, she was so sweet. You mustn't separate them, Mrs. Fielding. I think he needs her."

Julie had cut her short at that point. How dared this stranger tell her what was good for her boy?

But what if the dog was really helping him?

Then a girl called Jenny phoned.

"He's asleep," Julie said.

"I'm one of his friends," the girl with the English accent said. "Tell him I'm so happy he's going to keep Birdie."

One of his friends! Before they moved,

he had never had calls from one friend, let alone several.

Julie knew she should set the child straight, but somehow she could not get the words out. She went to the kitchen and put the chicken carcass on to boil for soup stock. She turned the heat to medium to get it started and went to make a grocery list. It was time she began cooking properly again. Dickon liked her homemade soup. She could bake bread too. He loved freshly baked bread.

She saw his face again. He had never looked at her like that before. Never. Her eyes filled with tears. Turning out the kitchen light, she picked up the newspaper on her way to her room. She undressed, propped herself up in bed, opened the paper and flipped through the pages. They seemed full of pictures of dogs, dogs and children playing, children and dogs in an ad for snowsuits. She felt battered by them.

In the kitchen the soup stock boiled fiercely. Next to the pot, a potholder that Julie Fielding had used earlier slipped from its hook and lay across the stove.

At ten, she sighed with relief. It was perfectly respectable to go to sleep at ten o'clock if you were tired. Never had she felt so weary.

Before she slept, she got out of bed and tiptoed into her son's room. His desk light blazed, his cheeks were tear-streaked, but at least he was sleeping soundly now.

"I'm sorry, Bird," she whispered, leaning to kiss him.

Out of the corner of her eye, she caught a movement and pulled back, startled. A plumy tail waved on the far side of the bed. The small dog did not growl now. She stood up, shook herself and held up a paw.

Julie stared.

Birdie looked reproachful and kept it extended.

Dickon's mother giggled.

"If I shake, it doesn't mean I promise to keep you," she told her son's dog in a whisper.

Birdie waited.

Timidly, Julie took the paw in her fingertips and shook it gently up and down. Birdie waved her tail like a flag of truce. Then she curled up beside her master and gazed up at the woman who had spoken of sending her away.

Laughing softly, almost hysterically, Julie left Dickon's bedroom and went to her own. For some time she lay awake. Finally, she picked up her diary and began to write. It did not take long to put down her surprising new thoughts. She stared at the page for a moment, put the diary back and was asleep in seconds.

It took over an hour more for the stockpot to boil dry. The pot grew hotter and hotter until the stovetop started to heat up as well and the potholder began to singe. The smell of scorched bones and a thread of smoke from the burning potholder stole across the kitchen and into the small hall.

Birdie awoke.

Yap! Yap! Whine! Yelp!

Dickon struggled half out of sleep.

"Stop that," he mumbled. "Birdie, shut UP!"

Birdie barked on. Dickon heaved himself up on one elbow and froze.

Smoke!

"Mum!" he screamed, leaping up and plunging into the hall. "Mum, FIRE!"

She was still asleep when he reached her. He shook her shoulder and screamed again.

"What?" she said.

Then she too smelled the smoke and the reek of the bones. She sprang up and all three of them raced to the kitchen.

Julie Fielding yanked the pot off the burner. She switched off the heat and hurled the smoldering potholder into the sink. Dickon turned the tap on. With a sizzle, the fire went out.

"What a mess!" she said, choking.

Birdie was racing around, as though she imagined they had all gotten up for a midnight jollification.

Julie turned to her son.

"Oh, Bird, how lucky that you wakened in time. You saved our lives."

Dickon's face glowed brighter than a Christmas tree.

"I didn't wake up," he said. "I was sound asleep. Birdie woke me. She kept barking, even after I told her to shut

up. I was mad until I smelled smoke. Birdie saved us. Birdie!"

His eyes were fixed on his mother's face. Surely now ...

She looked from him to his excited little dog.

"Come with me," she said and marched into her bedroom. Mystified, he followed. She flipped through the pages of her diary.

"Before you say another word, read this," she said.

Dickon looked at the page she was thrusting toward him. He did not want to read anything, but he made himself. It took him long moments to make out the words. Then his eyes widened. She had written, *I can't take that dog away from him. He loves her so. I have to let him grow up, just a little. Beginning with that dog ... if only she was not named Birdie.*

Dickon gave such a whoop of delight that, next door, Charlie put up her prickles in alarm. He flung his arms around his mother and hugged her until she was breathless.

"We could change her name," he offered, his eyes shining. "We could call her Wings maybe. But why don't we change mine instead? Why can't she be Birdie from now on and I'll be Dickon?"

There was a long silence. Finally, Julie Fielding reached out and rumpled his sleep-tousled hair.

"I'll try to call you Dickon," she said. "But it may take a while. Now go back to bed while I clean up."

Mrs. Nelson dropped by the next afternoon.

"My house might have gone up too," she said, stroking Birdie's tall ears. "Charlie and I are deeply grateful to you, sweet Birdie."

"Clever girl!" Dickon told his brave dog.

Then he remembered what Jody had said. Dogs were wonderful, but you had to take proper care of them. Give them exercise. He clipped Birdie's leash onto her collar.

"I'm taking her for a walk, Mum," he said offhandedly.

As he and Birdie went down the steps, he waited for his mother to warn him of every possible danger or to insist on coming with him. When she said nothing, he half-turned to stare.

"I'm so glad you're keeping the dog," Mrs. Nelson was saying. "She's not only brave, she's sweet."

"Well, she's here to stay – until I get a smoke alarm up anyway," Dickon's mother said.

Dickon's face paled before he saw that she was laughing.

"It's a joke, Dickon," she said.

He laughed too. Then, head high, he walked along the sidewalk, his dog heeling just as he had taught her. He was at the corner, looking both ways, when he took in what his mother had just said.

His dog would be Birdie forever. But he was no longer Birdie for now. His mother had done it.

She had called him Dickon.